Fire Wolf

The deadly hired killer Fire Wolf is heading to a remote set-tlement in answer to a telegraph message. On the way there he tangles with three wanted outlaws in the ghost town known as Gold Strike. When the remaining two outlaws show up they vow vengeance and trail the emotionless Fire Wolf.

Upon arriving in Jamesburg to find the man he thinks has hired his lethal services, it seems that no one is expecting him. No one apart from the actual man who has hired Fire Wolf.

Fire Wolf

Michael D. George

A Black Horse Western

ROBERT HALE

© Michael D. George 2018
First published in Great Britain 2018

ISBN 978-0-7198-2842-3

The Crowood Press
The Stable Block
Crowood Lane
Ramsbury
Marlborough
Wiltshire SN8 2HR

www.bhwesterns.com

Robert Hale is an imprint
of The Crowood Press

Typeset by
Derek Doyle & Associates, Shaw Heath
Printed and bound in Great Britain by
4Bind Ltd, Stevenage, SG1 2XT

PROLOGUE

Some might have called it a ghost town for it sure had the look of something only the dead might care to dwell within. A hundred buildings had crumbled beneath the merciless desert sun until only a mere handful still remained standing. The constant wind that came across the vast plains continued to batter what was left of Gold Strike. For nature has a way of reclaiming the land which men abandon and return it back to its genesis.

Gold Strike had had a brief yet lucrative history that ended as swiftly as it had begun. Some said a fortune in precious gold dust had been scattered across the desert by the incessant wind and the people who had originally been lured there simply followed it like mindless lemmings.

For more than a decade since the last of the town's inhabitants had left Gold Strike, the elements had relentlessly worked hard to destroy any evidence that the town had existed at all. Few men came to the desert settlement any longer and those that did were either lost or seeking a refuge from the law. No posse ever rode within a hundred miles of what remained of Gold Strike. The town had a reputation of being a good place to die and many had discovered the reality of that simple statement.

Yet as the blistering windswept sand kept eroding the handful of remaining structures beneath the brutal sun, a lone rider came out of the shimmering haze and steered his high-shouldered stallion straight at Gold Strike.

This was no ordinary horseman though. He was neither lost nor trying to avoid a hangman's knot. His journey to the remote settlement was quite deliberate. Unlike most drifters who rode across the perilous plains, the man in black knew exactly where he was and why he was there.

The rider was well aware that the abandoned town still had a dozen or more deep wells filled with precious water. A commodity that was far more valuable than a mountain of golden ore in this arid landscape.

The horseman had travelled this deadly route many times and knew that in total contrast to its appearance, Gold Strike had the purest water beneath its crumbling facades.

That was all he wanted. He would allow his mount to drink its fill and replenish his canteens before continuing his journey on to Jamesburg.

The ominous reputation that Gold Strike had for being a good place to die meant nothing to the expressionless rider as he neared the abandoned town. His trade was killing and death held no fear to him. His eyes narrowed as he cleared an outcrop of bleached white dead trees that resembled skeletons as they somehow remained upright.

His left hand drew back on his long leathers and stopped the grey stallion beside the lifeless trees as his keen eyes spotted three dishevelled horses tied up at the rear of what had once been a saloon. The saloon was one of the remaining buildings that had not been reduced to rubble.

Anger swelled up within the rider. He realized that the only men you ever met in this part of the desert were usually outlaws who tended to shoot at anything which moved. He exhaled and shook his head.

He bit his lower lip thoughtfully and then pushed the tails of his black topcoat over the grips of his holstered .45s. He could hear the raised voices of the horses' masters echoing from the interior of the saloon.

Without taking his intense stare off the sun-bleached building, he drew a long thin cigar from his inside pocket and bit off a half inch of its length and spat it at the white sand before him.

He knew that when Gold Strike had been abandoned it had been fast. So fast that its inhabitants had left practically everything within the structures. The saloon still had at least half its stock of hard liquor stacked upon its shelves beneath several inches of dust.

With the thought of getting his hands on just one of the whiskey bottles and downing its fiery contents, he struck a match and inhaled the strong smoke until his lungs were full of the toxic brew. He savoured its flavour for a few moments and then allowed it to seep between his gritted teeth as he tossed the spent match at the sand.

The cigar gripped firmly in his teeth, he leaned over the neck of the grey stallion and patted its lathered-up neck with his gloved land.

'I sure hope them varmints don't start shooting before I got time to kill them, Ghost,' he said drily before tapping his spurs against the sides of his horse.

The stallion proceeded on toward the remaining standing structures as the horseman flicked the safety leather loops off his gun hammers in anticipation of the forthcoming encounter.

There was an eerie silence as the handsome stallion moved between the piles of colourless rubble and headed into the wide street. His unblinking eyes scanned every one of the remaining structures as his spurs repeatedly nudged the flesh of the tall stallion. He glanced at the water trough outside the saloon and gave a muted chuckle. He relished the thought of encountering the three men that were still unaware of his arrival in Gold Strike. His sharp eyes did not blink as he continued to watch the open saloon door and listen to the drunken voices which filled his ears.

It had been over a year since he had last paid Gold Strike a visit and he noted the obvious changes. The saloon sign had fallen from its perch on the porch overhang and lay in countless fragments on the street sand.

The man in black glanced from beneath the black brim of his Stetson to where he was steering the tall grey. One of the original swing doors remained but was hanging by its hinge like a dead man on the gallows. The other had succumbed long ago to the elements and was nowhere to be seen.

The sound of the men's voices grew louder as the horseman turned his horse's head by a slight tug of his reins and headed straight at the water trough positioned directly outside the saloons still intact main window. As he pulled the long leathers up to his chest and stopped the animal, he heard the voices fade into silence.

A smirk etched his otherwise emotionless features.

'Reckon they seen us, Ghost,' he muttered as he threw his long right leg over the tail of his horse and slowly descended to the sand.

His left hand was still resting upon the saddle horn when he heard the hefty footsteps echoing through the saloon. They were moving toward the blazing sun-drenched street to see who Gold Strike's latest visitor was.

As smoke drifted up from the cigar between his teeth he caught sight of the trio of men as they stepped out beneath the porch overhang and paused on the boardwalk. They were a rough looking bunch who obviously by their appearance, and the stench which hung around them, had ridden hard to reach Gold Strike and the sanctuary the remote settlement offered.

The largest of the trio pushed between his cohorts.

'Who the hell are you, stranger?' Bart Hagen growled as he jabbed at the air with a stout finger. 'What you doing in these parts?'

The black-clad loner lowered his arm from the neck of the stallion, ignored the question and wrapped his reins around the water pump. He then gave the three men a brief glance and then started to prime the pump at the end of the trough. To the annoyance of the men standing on the boardwalk, he gave an amused smile and then felt the steel lever grow cold as water was drawn up from the depths and started to pour into the trough.

Another of the men edged closer to the lip of the boardwalk.

'Bart asked you a question, stranger,' Lex Smith shouted down at the man in black. 'Who are you?'

The youngest of the three, Cole Carver inched to Hagen's right and seemed less confident than his companions as he remained half hidden by his pal.

'And what in tarnation is you doing in these parts?' he chipped in sheepishly. 'Is you the law?'

The loner released his grip on the metal lever when he was satisfied that there was enough water in the trough to quench the stallion's thirst. He then slowly turned his tall frame and faced the three men.

'My name's Fire Wolf,' he uttered.

The faces of the three men seemed to drain of colour as the name sank into each of their minds. They had all heard of the last of the Mandan, but had never believed that he actually existed. Bart Hagen twitched as he bravely stepped forward until the toes

10

of his boots poked out over the edge of the board-walk.

'I heard about you,' he stammered.

Carver grabbed Hagen's sleeve and tugged it like a child trying to get its parent's attention. 'What is this varmint, Bart? Is he a bounty hunter?'

'I heard he was an Injun,' Hagen answered. 'But he don't look much like an Injun to me.'

'Me neither,' Smith agreed.

The face of the loner went grim as though he had just been insulted by their ignorance. His eyes narrowed until his entire face tightened.

'I ain't no stinking bounty hunter,' he hissed like a rattler and rested his hands on his holstered guns. 'I take exception to being called a bounty hunter. I'm Fire Wolf, the last of the Mandan.'

'What the hell is a Mandan?' Smith growled as his fingers slowly curled around his holstered six-shooter and he stared in disbelief at the disinterested man in black.

'He's come here after the bounty money on our heads, boys,' Carver said frantically. 'He's a blasted bounty hunter I tell you.'

Fire Wolf simply listened and watched.

Bart Hagen suddenly recalled the tales he had heard about the stranger in their midst. He wiped the sweat from his face and stared down at Fire Wolf in growing terror.

'You're wrong. He ain't no bounty hunter, Cole,' Hagen ventured as he placed his hand on his gun grip. 'He's a hired gun. A killer. I've heard about him

11

and what I've heard ain't exactly settling.'

There was a long silence as the three men under the overhang gathered their courage and stared down at the man in black who glared back at them. Finally, Cole Carver shuffled slightly forward and opened his mouth and spoke for what would be the last time.

'What kinda name is Fire Wolf?' he chuckled. 'I ain't no idea what a Mandan is, but is you a stinking Injun? Nothing I hates Injuns more than bounty hunters.'

Fire Wolf raised up to his full height as the outlaw's statement burned into him like a branding iron. His nostrils flared as he flexed his fingers above the ivory grips of his weapons.

'You shouldn't have said that,' Fire Wolf growled through the cigar smoke as his piercing stare burned across the distance between himself and the three wanted men.

Carver's expression suddenly altered. The mocking smile vanished as he realized that Hagen had not been exaggerating when he spoke about the man clad in black.

Fire Wolf spat his cigar at them and swiftly snatched both his weapons. With expert precision the hired gunman cocked the hammers of both weapons as they cleared the holsters and then aimed them straight at the dumbfounded outlaws.

They scrambled desperately for their guns, yet the trio of wanted men were no match for the infamous Fire Wolf. The ghost town shook as Fire Wolf squeezed his triggers with deadly determination. Blinding flashes spewed from the barrels of the guns. One of Fire Wolf's bullets hit Carver between the eyes and sent him flying backward through the saloon window. A thousand shards of glass splintered around the lifeless carcass of the outlaw's body as he hit the floorboards inside the saloon. Hagen fared little better as two shots carved a path into him. A plume of scarlet gore erupted from his chest, lifted him off his boot leather and punched him through the open doorway behind his wide back. No sooner had Hagen skidded to a halt beside the body of Carver than Lex Smith rocked on his feet as he held on to his Colt. His glassy eyes stared down in disbelief at the massive holes in his belly. Smith staggered and then toppled off the boardwalk toward the street. A plume of dust rose from the ground as the outlaw crashed face first into the sand before his executioner.

Fire Wolf stared at his bloody handiwork. There was no hint of emotion in his expression as he holstered his guns and glanced at the drinking horse. The animal had not even flinched during the deafening yet brief slaughter. It continued to drink from the trough beside its master. Fire Wolf ascended the saloon steps and entered the drinking hole through the gunsmoke cloud that hung over the bodies.

He moved across the vast empty expanse, where once bargirls plied their trade amid countless willing patrons, and moved behind the dust-covered bar counter. He glanced at the shelves of bottles hidden

13

ONE

The sky had reluctantly altered from blue into something that resembled the flames of Hell. Shafts of animated crimson hues spread across the heavens as day succumbed to the inevitable beckoning of night. Once it had been the very ground itself that was covered in rivers of flowing blood, but that had been before the weaker tribes had been crushed by the supremacy of their far stronger neighbours. Now it was only the vast sky that recalled the horrors of the past. Every night it would paint a vivid reminder of those lethal battles as if to warn the survivors that a far greater enemy was growing across the territory.

Entire tribes had been either slain or scattered to the winds by the violence between them. Even the victors had seen their numbers diminished until they were mere shadows of their former selves. Few, if any, of the various tribes could have imagined that a new danger was moving steadily through their lands. A constant flow of migrant settlers, flanked and protected by cavalry, were relentlessly heading westward in search of a better life.

They were drawn by the promise of a better life for themselves and their children and nothing could stop their advance. Had the warring Indians realized the volume of the encroaching settlers, they might not have battled one another but turned their attention to the far greater danger that grew like a cancer and would prove unstoppable.

Fire Wolf was one of the last of the northern Mandan tribe and had survived the wars that had destroyed most of his people by his superior wits. With a determination and grit that few could equal, Fire Wolf had managed not only to survive but also prosper.

He had learned that his hunting prowess had a value in the world of the white men. They would pay him handsomely to kill for them and Fire Wolf had no objections in killing.

As far as Fire Wolf was concerned, he was the last of his kind. Killing those who were not Mandan had never troubled the intrepid loner.

The solitary horseman steered his tall pale stallion through the barren range toward the distant outcrop of wooden structures set on a high rise between countless trees. His eyes glanced upward as he cleared his throat and intently absorbed the surrounding area. He spat out a hundred miles of accumulated dust at the ground and thrust his spurs into the flesh of the grey.

The tall horse responded and quickened its pace as Fire Wolf leaned back against the cantle of his saddle. Being a hired killer was an occupation he had grown into due to his lethal skills, yet no matter how many men he had sent to meet their Maker, he was never satisfied.

A burning rage smouldered deep down in his innards like a pending volcanic eruption. A fury that some might have called madness, while others considered it to simply be the mark of a man who lived by dishing out death, washed around in his blackened soul.

No amount of killing had managed to quench his thirst.

Fire Wolf was utterly unique in the ever-expanding West. He loathed the white men who paid for his deadly services but also detested the various tribes of Indians who he blamed for the destruction of his own people.

Yet there was no remorse or guilt in Fire Wolf as he guided his grey stallion on toward the small settlement. He simply did as he was paid to do and that was that.

If there had been any humanity dwelling in the lone gunman it was now buried beneath the mountain of victims he had dispatched over the years. It was as if he were attempting to bring the dead of his people back to life by killing anyone who made the error of standing in his way. It had never worked though and this darkened his already black mood as he travelled from one bloody job to the next.

His mind drifted from where he was back to a time long ago when his people made the mistake of attempting to fight the far superior Lakota. The Mandan had been slaughtered and those who had survived were enslaved or simply managed to escape like Fire Wolf.

The stallion snorted and brought Fire Wolf's attention back to the range. The sky was no longer crimson and stars were valiantly attempting to break through the twilight above them as he pushed the Stetson back off his emotionless features and glanced around him.

Fire Wolf held on to his long leathers firmly and gritted his teeth. The fury still raged inside his chest as his grey eyes observed the buildings on the ridge.

His anger was a constant companion nowadays. Beads of sweat trailed down his tanned face and dripped into his bandanna as he jabbed his spurs into the body of the grey stallion.

Fire Wolf had become the very thing he hated.

He had become a hardened assassin. A creature who gave no thought to the pain he inflicted. Far more merciless than the warriors who had practically wiped out the northern Mandan years earlier.

The grey mount forced its way through the last of the tall range grass and started to make its way across the hard rocky sand toward its goal.

'Keep moving, Ghost,' he drawled in a low whisper. 'We're almost there.'

Fire Wolf learned long ago that the only way to survive in this hostile land was to shed all the trappings of being a Mandan and become like the rest of the drifters. Luckily for Fire Wolf, the transformation had been easy. With his hair neatly cut above his collar, his facial features had never betrayed him. He dressed like a white man and that gave him access to places where Indians were never permitted to enter.

Few ever dared to question why he was called Fire Wolf. They knew that to do so was to risk the wrath of his weaponry and cold-hearted nature. The last of the Mandan was known for his merciless killing of those who stood in his way for he feared no one and respected no law.

The starlight caught the edges of the wooden marker ahead of his mount. His cruel eyes focused on the crude sign as his grey neared it.

Fire Wolf dragged back on his reins and stopped the tall grey in its tracks. The loner stared down at the wooden marker before him. There was enough light for him to read the markings painted upon it.

'Jamesburg,' he grunted as his long fingers clawed a thin cigar from his coat pocket and bit off its tip. He spat at the wooden marker and grinned as his spittle ran down the crudely painted name. It dripped on to the sandy ground. 'Reckon we found what we were looking for, Ghost.'

The dust-caked horse snorted as though agreeing with its master as it felt the long leathers pulling its head up off the ground again.

Fire Wolf turned the reins and jabbed his spurs into the flesh of the stallion. The horse responded and started trotting.

In a land of so many lone horsemen, few it seemed came this way. His eyes stared at the sand between the town and his horse's hoofs. There were no hoof tracks to be seen apart from those left behind his exhausted grey stallion.

As the sky darkened even more, Fire Wolf could see one light after another suddenly appearing within the array of buildings along the ridge. He straightened up on his saddle, scratched a match across his saddle horn and then raised the cupped flame to the cigar between his teeth. He sucked the smoke deep into his lean frame and allowed it to linger in his lungs for a while before exhaling.

The smoke hung in the still air as he kept the muscular stallion moving on toward his goal. Fire Wolf had travelled a long way to this place.

As he closed the distance between himself and Jamesburg he began to catch the acrid scent of outhouses in dire need of lime in his flared nostrils. Then his keen hearing caught the sound of tinny pianos and guitars hanging in the air.

'Seems like Jamesburg ain't as dead as it looks, Ghost,' he muttered through cigar smoke before adding. 'Not yet anyway.'

TWO

Jamesburg was not exactly what Fire Wolf had expected as his tall grey cleared the ridge and entered the lantern-lit settlement. From the range it had appeared to be nothing more than a scattering of wooden structures, like countless other towns he had visited during his journeys, but on closer inspection, it was large. Far larger than he had even imagined when he had accepted the job of hiring out his lethal skills to the man named on the telegraph message in his billfold.

Jeb James was a name that meant nothing to the lethal killer but that was nothing unusual to Fire Wolf. He had seldom met any of his clients before they contacted him by wire and hired him to do their bloody handiwork for them. Even as cigar smoke drifted around his wide-brimmed Stetson, he still did not question that it had been James who had telegraphed him.

The tall grey stallion was nervous beneath its master and danced in the amber light, but the man in black held his long leathers firm as he pondered the street ahead of him. He lashed the tails of the reins against the skittish animal and forcibly brought it under control.

'Easy, Ghost,' he ominously drawled. 'I don't cotton to crowds either. They trouble me.'

Fire Wolf sat astride his grey and screwed up his eyes as they studied the street before him. He eased back on his long leathers and blew a line of smoke at his gloved hands gripping his reins tightly.

This was no town like the one he had passed through a few days earlier. Jamesburg had a sense of permanence that was rare in this part of the territory. Even the amber flickering coal tar lights could not disguise that from the well-travelled rider in black.

More than half of the buildings were either constructed from brick or stone. They were made to last far longer than the folks who frequented its streets.

The sound of music blended into a senseless noise as it flowed from the open doorways of the saloons along the main street. Fire Wolf plucked the cigar from his lips and tapped the ash from what remained of its length as he attempted to control his temper.

Even the thought of folks actually enjoying themselves made no sense to the horseman. He ran gloved fingers across the .45 on his right hip and fought the desire to draw it from its holster and start killing. But not even Fire Wolf was reckless enough to start shooting with so many witnesses.

The horse pawed at the ground as its master continued to survey the long street of well-built structures. The stallion snorted its displeasure.

Fire Wolf pushed his hat off his furrowed brow and stared at the sky. Countless stars flickered in the heavens like precious diamonds on a cloth of black velvet.

The frustrated horseman returned his attention to what was before him. He could see two hotels of equal stature as well as at least four saloons dotted between scores of stores. His eyes tightened as he noted a half-dozen saddle horses tethered to hitching poles along the wide thoroughfare and about fifty men wandering between the various saloons.

'We gotta locate Jeb James and find out who he wants killed, Ghost,' Fire Wolf muttered to the anxious mount. 'I don't hanker after staying in this damn town a minute longer than necessary. A man could go deaf.'

It appeared to the deadly observer that all of the stores situated along the main street were open for business. That seemed strange to Fire Wolf. Their lantern light splashed out from their equally large windows from both sides of the street and nearly met in the centre of the sandy street.

Fire Wolf was surprised.

He was used to riding into a town, executing his nominated prey and then riding off into the sunset with his pockets full of cash. Jamesburg was no ordinary range town though. He sucked the last of the smoke from his cigar and then dropped it on to the sand before tapping his spurs into the flanks of the grey.

The powerful stallion started to walk slowly. Shadows and lantern light alternated and graced the horse and its thoughtful master as they travelled along the main street.

Fire Wolf was totally confused by the place he had ridden into. He knew that it would take time to locate the man who had hired him and even longer to find the elected victim. This town was far larger than it had appeared from down on the range and seemed to be getting larger the more his eyes studied it.

Side streets nearly as large as the main street splintered away from the busy middle of town. Fire Wolf tilted his head and noticed even more saloons and stores along their confines.

The brutal anger which was a constant companion to the man clad entirely in black festered in his innards. He wanted to kill and leave as he always did but knew that would not be possible in Jamesburg.

Then his attention was drawn to a sign hanging from a porch two hundred yards along the street. One simple word was painted upon it and it read: Sheriff.

Fire Wolf had even less respect for men who wore tin stars as they always poked their noses into things the lethal hired killer thought was none of their business. He spat at the ground as the grey passed by one of the numerous saloons. The aroma of a saloon was unmistakable. The mixture of sweat, spilled liquor and stale perfume had the ability of drawing even a blind man to its hallowed walls.

24

A thought occurred to Fire Wolf. Whoever Jeb James was, somebody in a saloon might have heard of him or be able to point the merciless killer in the right direction so that he might find his elusive paymaster.

His gloved hands eased back on his long leathers as they turned the grey toward the hitching pole. Two saddle mounts blocked most of the pole's length as the horseman stopped the stallion at its very end. Fire Wolf listened to the noisy goings on and stared with venomous eyes into the busy interior.

He looped his leg over the cantle and slowly dismounted.

The tall man in the black trail gear moved to the hitching pole and tied his reins securely to it. Fire Wolf stepped up on to the boardwalk and glanced up and down the busy street in search of anyone who might pose a problem to the ruthless hired killer. His eyes tightened as they fixed upon the sheriff's office and the light that cascaded from its window on to the sandy street.

Fire Wolf watched the shadows that passed across the window light and nodded to himself. He knew that at least one lawman was inside the building. He sighed then turned on his heels and moved toward the swing doors until his impressive height allowed him to have an uninterrupted view into the saloon as his mind raced. Tobacco smoke hung about five feet above its sawdust and the heads of the countless folks within it.

'Jeb James might be in there for all I know,' he

whispered to himself. He placed both hands on the top of the swing doors and pushed them apart and entered. Nobody noticed the arrival of the stranger as he stepped forward and stopped, but he noticed them.

Each and every one of them.

The sound of the doors rocking on their hinges behind his wide trail coat were drowned out by the multitude and an out-of-tune piano somewhere deep within the heart of the smoke filled drinking establishment.

Fire Wolf gritted his teeth as his fists clenched above his holstered six-shooters. The lantern light flashed across the gun's ivory grips that poked out from under the long black trail coat.

His calculating eyes flashed around the room. He made a mental note of every one of their faces as they drank and made merry. Not one of them seemed aware of Fire Wolf as he tightened the kid gloves over his hands.

He wondered if any of the saloon's customers were sober enough to know if Jeb James was anywhere close, but then he spotted the females.

In all his days he had never encountered a bargirl who could remotely be described as drunk. The females would encourage the menfolk to buy them drinks, but although the men would pay whiskey prices, the girls usually had only cold tea in their glasses.

A wry smirk etched his lean features.

Fire Wolf watched as nine scantily dressed bargirls

moved between the customers carrying trays of glasses to seated men dotted around the saloon. Then he observed their skilful antics as they tried to tempt them with their considerable wares.

The man in black stood watching as his hands extracted a cigar from its hiding place and bit off its tip before spitting at the sawdust and placing it between his teeth.

His fingers searched his pockets for a match when suddenly a lighted one was raised to the cigar by a long naked arm. His eyebrow raised as his eyes located the owner of the slender limb. He nodded in appreciation and puffed as his eyes travelled to the female stood beside him.

She then lowered her arm and blew the flame until all that remained between her fingers was a blackened ember. The tall man in black studied her in detail as he savoured the smoke inside his lungs. Mary Scott was a female who could have been aged anywhere between fifteen and thirty, he reasoned. It was impossible to tell for sure as her face was caked in unflattering make-up like the rest of the females in the saloon.

'I'm obliged,' Fire Wolf said as his eyes returned to the bustling crowd again. Mary edged closer to the stranger until her reinforced bosom pressed into him. He did not appear to notice or if he did, there was no reaction in his emotionless face.

'I ain't seen you before,' Mary said in a seductive manner as she circled the stationary stranger. Then her eyes noticed the guns at his side. The ivory grips were nothing like the ordinary wooden ones she had ever seen before. She knew that whoever the tall stranger was, he was dangerous. That excited her. 'I'd have remembered a handsome critter like you.'

Fire Wolf said nothing as his eyes narrowed against the tobacco smoke until they located the bar counter forty feet from where he stood.

The fingers of her left hand stroked his chest.

'Are you a gunfighter? '

His eyes flashed at her and then returned to the bar counter hidden in the foggy tobacco smoke. Fire Wolf did not speak as he concentrated on his objective.

Mary pressed herself into him with even more determination in a bid to try and gain his interest. Her hands kept wandering, yet he did not appear to notice.

'Are you looking for some company, good looking?' she purred seductively.

Fire Wolf again said nothing as his long legs started toward the distant bar counter. It was not an easy walk as the room was congested with men and females and none of them seemed aware of his ambition to get to the bar.

With every step, Mary remained at his side as her hands groped him in a vain bid to get a reaction. The hired gunman seemed oblivious to her provocative advances as he shouldered his way through the crowd until he reached his goal. He placed a boot on the counter's brass rail and then looked at the cowhands to either side of him. They were making it very difficult for him to catch the attention of the bartender as they nudged him from both sides.

Fire Wolf wanted more room but the liquored-up cowboys were not going to move aside willingly. He tightened the kid gloves over his large knuckles and then inhaled deeply.

As Mary caught up with the man in black, she saw his hands move swiftly to either side. His fists were clenched as they connected with the jaws of the drinking cowboys. The sound of his punches filled the large room as his knuckles jerked their heads violently backwards. As the cowboys started to fall unconsciously to the sawdust-covered floor, Fire Wolf grabbed their shirt collars, brought their heads together until they collided. Blood erupted from their faces and hung in the air for a few moments before they fell to either side of the man in black.

Fire Wolf kicked them into the sawdust and then stepped into the void left in their wake by the bar counter. Mary stepped beside the tall hired gunman. Her beautiful eyes dashed between the bloody cowhands curled up in the dust and the expression-less face of Fire Wolf as he in turn stared at the pair of men serving drinks.

There was no sign of any regret on the hardened features of the man in black for what he had just done to the drunken cowboys. It was as though he had just swatted some annoying flies and had already forgotten his brutal deeds.

Fire Wolf placed both gloved hands on the wet bar

counter and stared at the closest of the two bartenders. As their eyes met, the bartender suddenly
felt a terror racing through him like nothing he had
ever experienced before. He started to visibly shake
as he cautiously moved toward the deadly customer
and was thankful for the width of the mahogany
counter that separated them. The bartender had
never seen anyone floor two muscular cowboys so
easily before and it frightened him.

The bartender cleared his throat and mustered
every scrap of his courage in order just to be able to
speak to the grim faced Fire Wolf.

'W . . . what can I do for you, stranger?' he stammered.

Fire Wolf spread his fingers and rested his weight
on his hands. His unblinking eyes burned into the
nervous bartender with an almost hypnotic power.

'I want information,' he drawled. 'I reckon you
can provide that information. '

For eight years Heck Randle had worked as a bartender in every saloon in Jamesburg and knew a lot
more about its inhabitants than most. Yet he felt a
sudden dread filling his every sinew as Fire Wolf continued to stare at him.

'I ain't as smart as you reckon I am, stranger,' he
said as he steadied himself against the wooden
counter. 'I'll try to help you though, if I'm able. What
do you wanna know?'

Fire Wolf pulled the smouldering cigar from his
lips and exhaled a line of smoke at the damp
counter. He straightened up to his full impressive

height and then returned the smouldering cigar to the corner of his mouth.

'I'm looking for an *hombre* named Jeb James,' Fire Wolf answered grimly through a cloud of cigar smoke. 'Do you happen to know where I might find him?'

Randle was now even more nervous than before. The tall stranger terrified him, but the bartender knew that it did not pay to say anything about Jeb James. This was James' town and it was rumoured that he owned every living thing within its boundaries.

The frail bartender shrugged.

'Mr James could be anywhere in town,' he started. 'He practically owns Jamesburg.'

The answer surprised Fire Wolf. 'He owns Jamesburg?'

'Practically,' the bartender repeated.

Fire Wolf rubbed his gloved thumb thoughtfully against his chin. For the first time since he had entered the impressive settlement he started to realize that the man who had sent for him was a lot more than just another revenge-seeking client. The man in black tossed a couple of silver dollars on the counter and pointed at the array of whiskey bottles on a shelf behind the frightened bartender.

'If you see him, tell James that Fire Wolf is here,' the tall stranger said.

All the bartender could do was nod as the name was slowly absorbed into his mind.

The man in black pushed Randle towards the

stacked bottles on the shelf and pounded a fist on the counter.

'Now give me a bottle of your best whiskey, *amigo*,' Fire Wolf demanded coldly. 'One with an unbroken seal.'

'A bottle of whiskey,' the bartender repeated. He then did exactly as he was instructed and placed a bottle and glass down before the hired killer. Fire Wolf was about to pick up the bottle when Mary's slender arm darted at the vessel of amber liquor. She snatched it and held it to her ample cleavage.

Fire Wolf glanced down at her. He said nothing as she fluttered long lashes at him.

'I got us a nice quiet place to sip on this whiskey,' she said with an impish wink. 'Follow me.'

Heck Randle mopped his sweating face with his white apron and backed away from the counter as his fellow bartender took his place near the man in black.

Fire Wolf knew that he would not be getting any further information concerning Jeb James tonight. He was just thankful that the man who had apparently sent for him, actually existed.

His attention reverted back to Mary. His eyes stared at her clutching his whiskey bottle to her powdered breasts. He lifted the glass off the counter top as she turned and started to walk away from the bar.

Without uttering a solitary word, he began to trail her satin dress through the crowd to the staircase at the side of the bar counter. His emotionless expression gave no hint of what was brewing in his cold-calculating mind as he watched her swaying bustle and followed it toward the steps like a salmon attracted to a colourful lure.

Mary paused for a moment until the man in black caught up with her. She lifted her petticoats and ran halfway up the steps and then turned and looked down at him.

'Come on, handsome,' she said waving the whiskey bottle between them.

Fire Wolf chewed on the cigar and then slowly ascended the steps behind her. He said nothing as he followed her swaying dress up to the landing. When he reached the top step he silently turned and stared down at the assembled townsfolk below him and then returned his attention to the female.

'Where we going?' he asked in a hollow tone.

Mary raised her eyebrows in surprise. 'You can talk. I was starting to think that you only spoke to bartenders.'

His narrowed eyes glanced around the landing.

'Where we headed?' Fire Wolf asked.

'To my room of course,' Mary replied, waving the whiskey bottle before him as she ran around the balcony to the front of the saloon. Several doors faced her as she turned and watched Fire Wolf walking slowly toward her. The sound of his spurs echoed off the vaulted ceiling. Mary giggled and backed away from the deadly hired gunman. 'I got me a real soft bed.'

Soft beds did not impress Fire Wolf. He had been a grown man before he had even seen a bed let alone slept in one. His eyes glanced over the railings down at the large interior of the saloon and its continued revelry.

'You sure are a strange'un, handsome,' Mary remarked.

'You might be right,' he remarked as he momentarily paused to study the tobacco smoke-filled room below the landing. His attention was drawn back to the female as he heard the sound of her hand turning the door knob to her room.

Fire Wolf swung on his heels and watched as she opened a door and gestured for him to follow her into the room. He resembled an undertaker marching as he passed her and entered the room, leaving only a smoke trail hanging in the air behind the cigar gripped in his teeth.

The lantern lights from the street flooded through the painfully thin drapes and filled the room with amber illumination.

As Mary closed and bolted the door, she noticed the tall man stride past the bed to the window and look down at the main street and his grey stallion.

Mary jumped on the soft mattress with the bottle in her grip and looked at him. She patted the mattress beside her but Fire Wolf totally ignored her obvious invitation. He continued to study the street.

Totally bemused, she stared at her mysterious guest.

'What you looking at?' she asked.

He briefly glanced at her before returning his

attention to the window. Fire Wolf sighed as his left hand held the drape against the top window pane.

'I asked you a question,' Mary repeated as her petite hands worked on the cork and endeavoured to extract it from the neck of the bottle. 'What in tarnation are you looking at?'

'My horse,' Fire Wolf replied before removing his black hat and resting it upon the brass bed-knob. 'I was looking at my horse.'

Fire Wolf grabbed the bottle from her and pulled its cork with his teeth before returning his cigar to the corner of his mouth. He gave the open bottle back to her and then tossed the glass on to the bed.

As she filled the glass with the fragrant whiskey, the light from the street caught her large eyes. 'Why were you asking about old man James?'

'You know this Jeb James varmint?' he drawled as his eyes flashed at her.

For the first time since she had set eyes upon the mysterious stranger, Mary began to realize that Fire Wolf was far darker than she had first imagined. He was unlike any man she had ever encountered previously. Trepidation swept through the petite female sitting on the soft mattress.

'Yep, I know him.' She gave a slow nod of her head and then downed the strong liquor. Her expression told the hired gunman that she was not used to hard liquor. She coughed but repeated the action hastily to calm her nerves. 'Why'd you wanna find that old bastard?'

Fire Wolf glanced at Mary as he towered above her

tiny form. Even the shafts of lantern light that filtered through the gaps in the drapes could not
disguise his humourless expression from her eyes.

'I'm looking for him,' Fire Wolf stated. 'I've
ridden a long way coz he sent for me. I've kept my
part of the bargain and intend that he keeps his.'

He drew one of his six shooters and started to
reload its cylinder from the bullets on his belt. Fire
Wolf was silent as his nimble fingers continued to
pluck spent casings from his weapon's chambers and
replace them with fresh bullets.

No matter how hard she tried, she was unable to
read this man the way she normally did with her
clients. She filled the glass again and downed its contents.

'So you're here on business?'

He shrugged. 'You might call it business.'

Every instinct warned Mary Scott to stop questioning the dangerous stranger who she had locked into
the room with her, but the whiskey had other
notions. It had loosened her tongue and she was
helpless to prevent it from wagging.

'Now, what kinda business would you be in
Jamesburg for?' she wondered aloud before giggling
as she topped up her glass with more of the strong
drink. 'You sure ain't a drummer trying to sell folks
hard rock candy.'

Fire Wolf's eyes flashed at her. He did not respond
to her questioning. His merciless mind had other
thoughts that dominated his attention. Thoughts
that troubled the hired killer more than he cared to

admit. He wondered where the elusive Jeb James was and if it had been him who had sent the telegraph message at all.

Then Mary said something that drew his full attention.

'Are you a gunfighter?' she asked.

His poker face gave no clue to his companion that she had hit the nail on its head. Fire Wolf snapped the chamber of his gun back into the body of his six-shooter. For a brief moment he toyed with the weapon as he glared down at the giggling bargirl. Her watery eyes watched as he expertly twirled the .45 until it slid back into the holster. She then sighed heavily in relief as he paced back to the window, drew its drape and looked down at the still busy street below. Without turning his face away from the window, he sighed. The glass pane steamed up as his words hit its surface.

'Nope,' he finally answered drily. 'I'm a hired killer. Jeb James sent for me to do his killing for him. Least ways I think it was him who sent for me.'

The brief uttering made Mary stop laughing. A cold chill engulfed her as she suddenly realized that she had locked herself into her room with a killer. She rubbed her powdered throat as a bead of sweat rolled down her face. A droplet of sweat fell from her jaw and vanished into the canyon between her breasts.

'You're just joking,' Mary said quietly. 'Right?'

Fire Wolf looked over his wide shoulder at her.

'I never joke,' he stated.

THREE

The main street of Jamesburg resounded with the footsteps of the bartender as Heck Randle raced along the various boardwalks toward the small sheriff's office at a pace only frightened folks could ever attain. Upon reaching the structure, the bartender grabbed the door knob and swiftly entered.

Both the sheriff and his deputy looked up from behind their desks at the sweating face of the bartender as he closed the door behind him and stared out into the amber illumination as though terrified that he had been followed.

He was panting like a hound dog after a long hunt.

'What in tarnation are you doing, Heck?' Sheriff Dobie asked as he lowered his tin cup from his lips and rested it on his ink blotter. 'You almost made me choke on my coffee.'

Deputy Slim Baker had been awoken from a deep sleep and stared through sore eyes at the fearful bartender. 'You looks like you just seen a ghost, Heck.

38

What's wrong?'

'What I just seen was worse than any ghost,' Randle swallowed hard and then turned to face the lawmen who were staring curiously at him. He cautiously stepped toward the sheriff's desk and then rested his knuckles on its edge.

'Spill it, Heck,' Dobie said. 'What you seen?'

'There's a stranger in the Buckweed, Sheriff,' he exclaimed as sweat dripped from his bowed head upon the wooden desk like rain.

Dobie moved his coffee cup closer to him and then stood. He had never witnessed the bartender so obviously terrified before and that alone troubled him.

'Is that why you're so all fired up, boy?' the sheriff asked as he placed a hand on the arm of the shaking Randle. 'Saloons are bound to draw strangers now and again. Calm down.'

Randle tilted his head and looked into the comforting face of the older lawman. He shook his head.

'You ain't seen this dude, Sheriff,' he stammered. 'He just don't look like regular folks. I thought he was going to kill me.'

Sheriff Dobie stroked his whiskers and glanced across at his deputy as he patted the trembling bartender in a fatherly fashion.

'There ain't no call for you to be so damn scared, boy,' he sighed as Randle turned and rested his rump on the edge of the desk. 'Jamesburg is mighty peaceful most of the time but now and again we get folks that ain't exactly easy on the eye.'

39

The bartender inhaled deeply and then looked the veteran lawman straight in the eye.

'He said his name was Fire Wolf, Sheriff,' Randle blurted as he continued to look at the office door as though in fear of the last of the Mandan catching up with him. 'Fire Wolf the hired killer.'

The deputy chuckled from behind his desk.

'Fire Wolf? What kinda name is that?' he laughed.

Sheriff Dobie raised a finger and silenced his deputy before moving around the sweat-soaked bartender. Like the terrified man, he had also heard of the name.

'Are you sure he said his name was Fire Wolf, Heck?' he asked as he felt his heart pounding beneath his shirt.

Randle just nodded.

'You couldn't have misheard him?' Dobie pressed.

The bartender sighed and then wiped the sweat from his face as he somehow managed to control his terror for a brief moment. He grabbed the forearm of the veteran lawman and forced Dobie to look directly into his eyes.

'You gotta believe me, Sheriff,' he pleaded. 'That's the name that he give me. Fire Wolf.'

Dobie rubbed his jaw.

'So the varmint actually exists,' the sheriff muttered to himself and suddenly felt a chill race up his spine. He moved to the door and placed the palm of his left hand upon its glass panel as he stared out into the artificial illumination.

The deputy had never seen his mentor like this

40

before and got to his feet before moving to the pot belly stove and warming his hands. Baker looked between the bartender and the sheriff for a few moments before walking across the boards to where Dobie was deep in thought.

'You ain't giving this any credence, are you?' he whispered in the ear of his superior. 'Heck is just liquored up.'

Randle looked up at the deputy.

'I ain't drunk and I ain't deaf either, Slim,' the bartender said in his defence. 'I just served Fire Wolf with a bottle of whiskey.'

Dobie pushed himself away from the door and stared at the obviously troubled bartender.

'What's he look like, boy?' he asked.

Mustering every scrap of his composure, the bartender stood and raised his hand to demonstrate the height of the stranger he had encountered.

'He stood about this tall, Sheriff,' Randle explained. 'He was way taller than me and I'm close to six foot. He was dressed all in black and never once smiled. It was like looking into the face of death.'

Slim Baker screwed up his face. 'That's awful tall for an Injun, ain't it?'

Both Dobie and Randle looked at the deputy.

'What you talking about, boy?' the sheriff growled.

'Ain't Fire Wolf an Injun?' Baker queried in confusion. 'He sure sounds like an Injun with a name like that.'

Randle was shaking. 'That *hombre* don't look like

any Injun I've ever seen, Slim.'

Sheriff Dobie returned to his chair and sat down. He sighed and leaned back. His mind was racing as he tried to recall everything he had ever heard about the infamous hired killer.

'Fire Wolf ain't an ordinary Injun like the kind we're used to, boys,' he started to explain. 'I heard tales that he is the last of his kind. A tribe that I believe was called the northern Mandan. They were a strange bunch by all accounts. Some even reckoned that they were not pure Injuns at all, but part Welsh or something like that. I heard stories that they didn't look like any of the other tribes.'

'Welsh?' Baker scratched his jaw. 'What's that?'

'It's like Scottish only different,' Randle explained.

The sheriff cleared his throat and drew their attention again. He continued.

'Maybe it's just a tall tale, but they reckon a Welsh prince and his cronies come to America long before the other settlers showed up.' Dobie lit his pipe and puffed a few times before pointing its stem at the dubious deputy. 'Fire Wolf apparently survived the Injun wars which wiped out most of his people. God knows what happened to him after that but whatever happened it sure didn't mellow him none.'

Randle looked down at the seated lawman.

'I heard stories that he's a heartless killer, Sheriff,' he said.

Slim Baker could hardly believe what he was hearing.

'The critter sounds plumb loco to me,' he said.

Dobie gave a nod of his head as smoke billowed from his mouth. He sighed heavily and placed his hands together as though in prayer.

'Whatever happened to Fire Wolf when he was younger must have branded him for life,' he said. 'He's said to be nothing but pure hatred. What other kind of critter would kill folks for a living? I've heard that he'll kill anyone with equal relish. It don't matter none to him. He just kills.'

'Even women?' the deputy gasped.

'Even women, Slim,' Dobie shrugged.

'Holy smoke,' Baker exhaled, marched to his desk and picked up a bundle of Wanted posters and began thumbing through them. 'When I find a poster with his name on it, I'll go round him up.'

Dobie sat forward. 'Are you eager to die, Slim?'

The deputy looked at his superior. 'What you mean, Sheriff?'

Dobie extracted the pipe stem from his lips and then pointed it at Baker. He sighed and shook his head.

'You won't find any Wanted poster with Fire Wolf printed on it, boy,' he stated knowledgeably. 'That varmint ain't wanted for nothing.'

The deputy and the bartender were equally shocked by the statement. Neither of them could imagine that anyone could do so much killing and not be wanted. The young lawman stared straight at the sheriff.

'But you said he's a known killer,' Slim Baker

looked totally bemused as he placed the posters back down.

Dobie nodded firmly. 'So he is but you try and prove it, Slim. He's as deadly as they come, but nobody has ever managed to pin anything on him.'

The bartender accepted a cup of coffee from the deputy and then looked through its steam at the sheriff. He blew at the hot beverage and stammered.

'Is he a bounty hunter?' he asked. 'Is that how he has done so much killing and gotten away with it?'

Dobie grinned. 'Nope. The last of the Mandan ain't no stinking bounty hunter, Heck. He's a hired gunman. Fire Wolf sells his services to anyone who can meet his price. He does what most folks would never even entertain. He kills for a price and then moves on to his next paymaster and potential victim.'

'And we can't pin nothing on him?' Baker piped up.

Dobie shook his head and then returned the pipe stem to him mouth and puffed heartily. 'Nope, we can't. Just think about, boys. Who would dare to get on the wrong side of the infamous Fire Wolf? That would be plumb suicidal.'

The deputy was still young enough to think that he was better than most folks with his gun. Baker had not lived long enough to learn that there was always someone faster with their gun, and to discover that the good do not always win against the bad.

'Fire Wolf is just a man,' he snarled. 'I ain't feared of no man, Sheriff.'

Dobie nodded.

'I know you are, Slim,' he said. 'but that don't mean you could get the better of someone like Fire Wolf. That varmint has spent most of his life killing. Folks like us think about our actions but someone like him never gives it a second thought. That second is the difference between life and death.'

'He's real mean-looking, Sheriff,' Randle stated as he sipped at the coffee. 'His eyes were lifeless. It was like looking into the eyes of a critter who was already dead.'

The sheriff rubbed his white whiskers thoughtfully.

'Why is he in Jamesburg?' Dobie wondered aloud.

The bartender knew the answer to that simple question. He lowered his cup from his face.

'He's looking for Jeb James,' Randle said. 'He even asked me where he was.'

Both lawmen glanced at one another and then returned their full attention to Randle. Dobie got to his feet and circled the desk to where the bartender was standing. He poked the pipe stem into his belly.

'Did Fire Wolf say why he was looking for Jeb, boy?' the sheriff asked.

Randle shook his head. 'He never said nothing apart from he was looking for Jeb, Sheriff. I told him that I didn't know where he was. That seemed to rile him.'

'Now that is mighty curious,' Dobie muttered as he considered the bartender's words carefully. 'Why would the notorious Fire Wolf show up here looking for the richest varmint in the territory?'

FOUR

Darkness hung over the vast desert terrain like a shroud as the sound of distant movement drew ever closer to the long abandoned Gold Strike. At first it was barely noticeable amid the bone-chilling howls of coyotes baying at the new moon. Then it grew more distinctive as the horsemen carved a route toward the remote settlement.

A scattering of defiant clouds hid the new moon from view and prevented its eerie light from illuminating the pair of riders as they continued to make their way to Gold Strike. Yet the sound of their spurs and saddles drifted on the night wind as though mocking the eyes of those who might have detected their forthcoming arrival.

Finally, the moon broke free of the fast-moving clouds. Its haunting light glinted off the frost-covered sand. Yet there were no human witnesses within miles of the deserted town to notice either the sight or the sound of the advancing riders.

The arid desert terrain had continued its slow

progress in destroying the ghost town of Gold Strike. Nightfall had brought a brief respite to the blistering temperature, which had already started its hideous destruction of the three corpses lying in and around the saloon. No sooner had Fire Wolf refilled his canteens with ice-cold water and ridden on toward Jamesburg, than vultures had appeared as if from nowhere and started to feast upon the bodies.

Ravenous vultures were not the only creatures ready to take advantage of either the dead or the dying, though. Drawn by the irresistible scent of blood, many other creatures had joined in the carnage to subdue their hunger.

It was only when the sun had eventually set that the large birds flew away from the bodies of the three outlaws. Their hooked beaks and dagger-like talons had mercilessly torn the corpses apart long before rigor mortis had stiffened their lifeless bodies. Blood and guts covered the saloons floorboards and bore evidence of the disgusting yet utterly efficient actions of the hideous vultures' actions.

No frantic fever-crazed maniac could have scattered the outlaws' remnants with more disdain. The light of the new moon cast its eerie illumination across the ghost town as the sound of horses' hoofs and bridles started to echo in the night air off the remaining structures' facades.

A lone coyote was the only witness to the arrival of the two horsemen who approached the abandoned settlement. The animal had barely had time to gorge on the entrails of the bodies when his senses alerted him to flee. The scrawny creature raced from the saloon with a lump of flesh hanging from its jaws. It kept on running until it found refuge.

Moonlight glanced across the pair of riders as they approached the outskirts of Gold Strike, giving them an almost surreal appearance. Yet these were no phantoms or mere imaginings. These were hardened outlaws who had earned the bounty upon their heads.

Just like the dead outlaws, they had sought out the remote settlement in order to find sanctuary from those who hunted them and to catch up with their three gang members in order to share the spoils of their latest outrage.

Lane Holden and Ben Allen carried two swollen canvas bags tethered securely to their saddle cantles. Both bags had the words El Paso Mutual Bank stencilled in bold letters across their widths.

'Where do you reckon the boys are, Ben?' Holden wondered as he gazed around the moonlit rubble. 'It's awful dark. There oughta be light showing from someplace.'

'You're right.'

Ben Allen had been wondering the same thing himself as he controlled his lathered-up mount who seemed unusually skittish the closer they rode to the handful of remaining structures. Then he noticed that Holden's horse was also straining at the bit.

'What's the matter with these nags?'

'They smell something,' Allen said. 'Something that makes them mighty nervous.'

'You're right, Lane,' Holden growled as he slid his .45 from its holster and rested it on top of his saddle horn. 'I'd have thought that the boys would have lit a few lamps once the sun set.'

'What spooks animals like this?' Allen wondered. 'Are we riding into a trap?'

'There's only one thing that spooks grown horse-flesh, Ben,' Holden said under his breath. 'The smell of death.'

Allen swallowed hard. He knew that his partner was probably right. He rubbed his dry lips with the back of his glove as they advanced into the heart of Gold Strike.

Lane Holden's eyes ached as he strained to see in the darkness. He eased back on his long leathers and stopped his mount twenty feet from the front of the saloon. Something on the sand close to the structure's boardwalk had caught his keen attention. As Allen halted his horse beside his partner, he watched Holden raise a finger and point.

'Do you see that?'

Allen started to nod. 'Yep, I see it but I can't figure out what it is.'

Holden sniffed the air and caught the acrid stench which was alarming the horses. He knew exactly what it was that he was looking at, but was loath to admit it, even to himself.

'Whatever it is, it's dead,' Holden said.

'Sure smells dead.'

The haunting moonlight tormented their dust-caked eyes and glinted off the fresh entrails that the coyote had torn from the savage wound created by numerous ravenous vultures during their feast. The mixture of frost and moonlight danced across the sand surrounding the carcass. Then suddenly something unexpectedly erupted from within the saloon and came flying straight at Holden. Both horses reared up and kicked out at the debris that enveloped them. Holden fell over the cantle of his saddle and hit the ground hard.

FIVE

Even though Holden was dazed by his spectacular fall, he still managed to hold on to his long leathers and prevented the terrified horse from galloping off into the darkness. With blood pouring from his nose he got back to his feet and hauled the wide-eyed animal into submission.

'What in tarnation was that, Ben?' the dazed outlaw gasped as he watched as his partner managed to subdue his own mount without being unseated from his saddle.

Allen fanned the choking dust from before his face and then focused on the ground a few feet from the mutilated body. Having gained control of his horse, he pointed down at two large black feathers lying upon the moonlit sand.

'It must have bin a buzzard or maybe even an eagle,' he reasoned wrongly as the large vulture flapped its wings above the ghost town.

Holden slapped his hat against his legs and then placed the trampled Stetson back on his head. He stared up at the star-filled sky and sighed heavily.

'That was a damn vulture, Ben,' he growled.

Allen slowly looped his leg over the wide horse and dismounted. He moved toward his winded friend and looked him over before satisfying himself that Holden was still intact.

'What do you reckon that bird was doing in there, Lane?' he asked pointing at the saloon.

'Eating,' Holden replied drily before handing his reins to his cohort.

The moonlight caught the fearful expression carved into the hardened features of Allen as he considered the brief yet shocking utterance. No matter how hard Allen tried to sanitise his thoughts, it was impossible. He knew deep in his guts that their fellow outlaws were already dead, but could not comprehend how that could be possible.

Hagen, Smith and Carver had all been dead shots just like Holden and himself. Allen stared at his partner in disbelief.

'Are you thinking what I'm thinking, Lane?' he asked.

Holden nodded. 'Reckon I am, Ben.'

Both men advanced closer to the saloon and the horrific sight of the mutilated outlaw that lay crumpled on the sand below the boardwalk steps.

The sickening smell grew stronger. Only the night frost that covered the body made it tolerable. There was no mistaking the fact that the body had been one of their fellow outlaws until only a few hours earlier. Yet it was impossible to tell which one it had been.

Holden glanced at his friend.

'Try and keep these nags from bolting, Ben,' he whispered as his index finger curled around his six-gun's trigger. 'I'll take a look inside in case there are any other surprises waiting for us.'

Allen gave a silent nod then led the two horses to the hitching pole and set about securing the animals' reins. There was still water in the trough which Fire Wolf had pumped into it hours earlier. Allen stood as the horses began drinking.

Holden cocked his gun hammer and then ascended the boardwalk steps. The outlaw reached the boardwalk, leaned against its weathered wall and screwed up his eyes. He peered into the saloon and then saw what was left of the two other bodies.

'I reckon I found the other boys, Ben,' Holden sighed heavily and looked down at Allen. 'They didn't fare any better that the galoot on the sand.'

Holden swung around on his heels and entered the deserted saloon. Every step echoed around the large interior as the outlaw ensured that he avoided the gruesome entrails that were scattered in all directions.

'I reckon I found out why that vulture was in here, Ben,' Holden called out over his shoulder. 'Come take a look at the mess I nearly stepped in.'

Allen sucked in his stomach, rested his hands on his holstered gun grips before moving along the hitching pole and then mounting the steps cautiously up the saloon entrance.

Even the darkness could not conceal the horror.

Allen rubbed his dry mouth on the back of his sleeve and then carefully entered.

'This is damn bad, Lane,' he muttered. 'These are our boys OK. I recognize their trail gear.'

'Yep, you're right, Ben,' Holden agreed with a sharp intake of breath. 'The one that came through the window is wearing a pair of fancy new boots. Cole bought himself new boots in El Paso before we robbed the bank there.'

Allen shook his head as he moved around the bodies just inside the saloon doorway. He still was having trouble accepting the fact that someone had killed the trio.

'I just don't understand it, Lane,' he blurted out pushing his hat off his brow. 'Who could have gunned these boys down like this?'

'Someone mighty fast on the draw, Ben,' Holden drawled.

'I'd have said that there ain't anybody that fast,' Allen growled in disbelief. 'These boys were the best. That's why we hired them. It just don't tally that someone could wipe them out like this.'

'I'm finding it hard to believe myself,' Holden said. 'All I know for sure is that whoever they tangled with was one mighty fine gunman.'

Shafts of moonlight cut through the gaps in the saloon's weathered walls and splashed across the horrific scene. After absorbing the sight which had greeted him, Allen glanced up to the equally stunned Holden.

'What the hell happened here, Lane?' he gasped

waving his hands at the bodies. 'Explain this to me. I just don't understand this.'

Holden straightened up to his full height.

'Me neither,' he admitted.

Holden turned away and marched across the floor to the dusty bar counter. He moved behind the bar counter and brushed cobwebs off a whiskey bottle. As he pulled its cork and took a long swig from the bottle's neck, Allen joined him.

'They must have bin bushwhacked,' Allen reasoned as he leaned upon the counter. 'Nobody could have bested them boys in a straight fight.'

'Cole was shot in the head,' Holden argued. 'Whoever shot him done that from the front. I reckon if you check Lex and Bart, they were also facing their executioner as well.'

Allen accepted the bottle and took a long swallow himself.

Holden scratched a match and lit a candle. Shimmering light illuminated the counter. The outlaw then located a lamp and gave it a shake. When satisfied that it had oil in its glass tank, he lifted its funnel and touched its wick.

Allen watched as Holden then proceeded to put flame to another few lamps. Within a few moments the large bar room was bathed in flickering light.

The amber illumination was disconcerting as it allowed the two men to see the bodies of their fellow outlaws more clearly and the dried gore that surrounded them.

Allen took a long drink of the whiskey as Holden

stared down at the floor. The lamplight revealed something which neither he nor Allen had noticed before.

'Look at the floor, Ben,' Holden snarled, pointing an accusing digit at the bloody footprints to and from the counter. 'See them boot prints?'

Allen looked down and then spotted the scarlet boot marks on the dusty floorboards. For a moment he thought that either he or Holden and stepped in the blood when they had entered the saloon, but then realized that the prints were dry. He looked up at Holden and pointed at the unmistakable trail left by the deadly Fire Wolf.

'These must be the boot prints of the varmint that killed our gang, Lane,' he declared before adding, 'As far as I can see there's only one set of marks. Holy smoke, there was only one bastard that shot our boys.'

'Just like I figured, Ben,' Holden nodded. 'The varmint that killed them boys ain't no normal gunman. He's gotta be faster than anyone we ever seen.'

'But who in tarnation could be fast enough to kill all three of them, Lane?' Allen asked fearfully. 'And why would anyone do that?'

'Why?' Holden sighed heavily. 'Because he could, that's why. Some folks just can't help but show what they can do.'

Ben Allen tightened his bandanna and tucked its tails into his shirt front, but it wasn't the night air that chilled the outlaw to the bone.

It was fear. He could not imagine that anybody would cold-bloodedly slaughter three men and then walk calmly to the bar and help himself to a whiskey bottle. His eyes noticed the half empty whiskey bottle at the end of the long counter. He moved toward it and noticed that the glass vessel had been wiped clean of cobwebs. Allen pointed at the bottle and drew Holden's attention.

'Look at this, Lane,' he said as the oil lamp's light danced across his nervous face. He lifted the bottle and studied it carefully. 'The seal on this bottle was only broken a little while back.'

Holden paced to his partner's side and stared long and hard at the bottle and its amber contents. Then he noticed a small thimble glass on the very edge of the dust-covered counter top.

'That glass there is clean, Ben,' he noted. 'That must be the one he used to do his sipping from.'

Allen placed the bottle back down and rubbed his sweating face as he stared down at the floor and shook his head over and over again.

'What kinda varmint is this?' he wondered.

Lane Holden rested his knuckles on his gun grips thoughtfully and considered what they had discovered. He tilted his head and looked at the other outlaw.

'Well, whoever killed our boys, it sure weren't a bounty hunter,' he reasoned. 'No bounty hunter would have left the bodies here to be torn apart by wild critters. Lex alone was worth $2,000. Together, I reckon they must be worth twice that amount. Nope, it sure wasn't a stinking bounty hunter that done for our boys.'

Allen began to nod in agreement.

'You're right,' he said. 'No bounty hunter would have left three valuable corpses to rot. He'd have taken them with him to claim the reward money.'

'Besides, have you ever heard of a bounty hunter brave enough to face the men he kills?' Holden spat at the floor. 'Most of their breed are back-shooters. They ain't got the grit to face their targets like real men.'

Allen nodded in agreement. 'Then who did this, Lane? Is there another kind of critter we ain't thought about? Someone who ain't scared by heavily-armed outlaws and has the guts to kill them like an *hombre* just swatting flies.'

Holden lowered the whiskey bottle from his lips and then glanced at Allen. His expression changed from one of anger to one of bemusement.

'I reckon I've heard tell of such an *hombre*, Ben,' he ventured. 'I heard stories but never paid them any heed as they sounded too far-fetched.'

Allen moved closer to his gun pal.

'What kinda stories and who is this *hombre*?' he pressed his thoughtful friend.

'There are a few black-hearted souls who hire themselves out to anyone who has their asking price,' Holden drawled. 'They'll kill anyone without giving it a second thought.'

Allen looked confused. 'But a hired killer wouldn't have shot our boys down like dogs. What makes you think it was a hired gunman that did this, Lane?'

'Not just any hired killer, Ben,' Holden corrected. 'The kind that don't just kill for money. I've heard of one man who is said to have no fear running through his veins like normal folks. He hates everyone and ain't blessed with humour like normal folks.'

'Who?' Allen asked as sweat ran down his face. He shook the cobwebs from a beer glass and then picked up the whiskey bottle they had been sharing. He poured three inches of the powerful amber liquor into it. 'Has he got a name?'

'Yep, he's gotta name OK.' Holden replied.

'Then what is this bastard called?'

Holden pulled out his tobacco pouch and started to sprinkle its contents on to a thin cigarette paper. As his teeth tightened the pouch's drawstring, his fingers rolled the tobacco-filled paper until it attained the correct shape. He returned the pouch to his vest pocket and then licked the gummed edge of the cigarette and placed it in the corner of his mouth.

'Have you ever heard of Fire Wolf?' he asked coldly.

Allen downed the whiskey in one long swallow. He gave a silent nod of his head and watched as Holden leaned over a candle flame and sucked smoke into his lungs. He had heard the name, but had never believed it belonged to a real man, thinking it was just a tall story.

There was a long silence until Holden rested his broad back against the counter and exhaled a line of smoke. He glanced at Allen and hissed through the billowing tobacco smoke.

'He's the only one varmint that I know of who would kill wanted men and then leave them to rot, Ben,' he said as he carefully plucked tobacco leaf off his tongue. 'Fire Wolf ain't nothing like normal critters. Nothing scares him.'

Allen narrowed his eyes.

'Nothing scares him?' he repeated.

Holden drew more smoke into his lungs and then blew it at the ceiling. His eyes darted back to Allen as the outlaw refilled his glass with whiskey.

'Nothing,' he confirmed.

'How d'you know so much about this critter?' Allen blurted as he stared at the smoking Holden.

Holden pulled the cigarette from his lips, flicked its ash and then returned it.

'When we were back in El Paso I heard tell of Fire Wolf. He's a lethal hired killer, a man that never gives a man a second chance.'

Allen rubbed his neck. 'I heard tell he's just a legend. No man could be as mean as him or done half of what he's said to have done without having his neck stretched.'

Holden shrugged. 'He might be real and he might just be a legend like you reckon, Ben.'

'So I reckon we'll be heading back to El Paso then,' Allen started to smile. 'I sure don't hanker to be chasing anyone as devilish like Fire Wolf. Even if he is a legend, I don't wanna meet the varmint.'

'We can't head on back to El Paso, Ben,' Holden

pointed out drily. 'Not until they forget what we look like and the fact that we just robbed the biggest bank there.'

'And killed half a dozen folks who tried to stop us,' Allen added before looking at his friend. 'I reckon you're right. They might get a tad tetchy if we go back there.'

Holden dragged the whiskey bottle across the dusty bar counter and stared at its meagre contents. Without complaining, he downed the amber liquor and then stared at the empty bottle in his hand.

Suddenly he tossed the bottle over his shoulder.

As it floated in the lamp light, Holden swung around on his boot leather, drew his .45 and fired. A flame and cloud of gunsmoke went flying through the air. The bottle shattered into a million fragments.

Before the countless pieces of glass hit the floor, Holden had holstered his still smoking gun and turned back to the counter.

Allen winced in pain and held his ears. His eyes darted at the silent outlaw until Holden looked at him.

'What in tarnation did you do that for, Lane?' Allen grumbled as his hands lifted his glass and downed half its contents. 'You could have warned me.'

Holden nodded in agreement. 'You're right. I could have warned you, but I was just proving a point.'

Allen stepped nearer the older man. 'What was you proving? '

'I'm also damn good with my guns, Ben,' Holden muttered and then walked around the counter and dragged another dusty whiskey bottle off its shelf and started to wipe the cobwebs off its surface.

Allen suddenly realized what was on Holden's mind.

'If we ain't heading back to El Paso,' he stammered. 'Which way are we heading, Lane?'

'When the sun rises we'll be able to tell which way the killer went after he slaughtered our boys, Ben,' Holden responded before drawing the cork from the neck of the bottle and spitting it across the room. 'We can follow him to wherever it is he rode to.'

'Are you loco?' Allen protested as he watched his partner take a swig from the bottle. 'You intend following Fire Wolf?'

'If it is Fire Wolf,' Holden teased. 'I might be wrong. It might be that some cowpoke got lucky and managed to kill all three of our boys, Ben.'

Allen pressed his hands on to the counter and glared at Holden. His face creased as he glared at the seemingly unconcerned outlaw.

'You seriously intend trailing the varmint that killed these boys?' Allen shouted as he waved his arm around like a hysterical windmill. 'What'll happen if we catch up with him?'

'Just imagine that if it is Fire Wolf we're trailing and he's hiring out his killing skills it could be very profitable for us,' Holden suggested. 'He probably gets paid about $10,000 for killing someone. All we gotta do is bushwhack him after he's been paid.'

'That'll be damn easy,' Allen exhaled and shook his head. 'All we gotta do is kill the most dangerous bastard in the territory and steal his loot. Simple.'

Holden nodded in agreement.

'I'll go get the bedrolls then,' Allen grumbled. 'I'll bring them canvas bags in as well.'

'Good idea,' Holden said as he lifted the bottle to his lips again and allowed the powerful liquor to burn its way down into his innards.

Allen marched away from the counter. He shook his head with every step that he took.

Holden watched the outlaw stride across the bar room toward the entrance and then disappear from view into the darkness. He then placed the bottle down and sighed heavily as he caught sight of his own reflection in the grimy saloon mirror. He stared at the distorted image.

'If you get this wrong,' he whispered to himself. 'You're gonna be just another notch on Fire Wolf's gun grip.'

SIX

A new moon and countless dazzling stars stretched across the heavens above the sheriff and his deputy as they rode the two-mile distance between Jamesburg and the wealthy rancher's lavish homestead. Set at the highest point of the long ridge, the massive stone and red brick house could be seen for miles from every direction. Yet it was not exactly what it appeared to be. The closer the pair of lawmen got to their destination, the more its secrets were revealed.

For some reason Jeb James had built himself a fortress.

A stone wall had been erected around the impressive house with sentry towers at four corners. A solid wooden gate blocked the trail in and out of the virtual stockade ominously ensuring that no uninvited guests got close to the main house.

Heavily armed guards were positioned on each tower and a further half dozen men patrolled the inner grounds between the wall and the house.

The imposing structure resembled a prison rather than a house. For whatever reason, Jeb James liked it that way and there was no one within a hundred miles who had ever had the courage to question why.

Like all those who had gone before them, both the lawmen felt as though they were approaching a place of execution rather than the residence of the wealthiest man in the territory. As Sheriff Dobie led his deputy ever closer to the imposing gates, he felt a bead of sweat trickle down his spine.

The lawman had been to this place many times over the years to inform Jeb James of the goings-on in the sprawling settlement, yet it was a journey he had never felt comfortable with.

Moonlight glinted off the long rifle barrels as well as the newly installed Gatling guns perched to either side of the gates on the towers.

'What in tarnation does Mr James want all them guns for, Sheriff?' the naïve deputy asked nervously. 'Seems like he don't want folks visiting him. How come?'

'Maybe he don't.' Dobie did not have the answers to any of the questions posed by his junior and had always thought it was safer that way. Whatever Jeb James did was none of his business, he thought. Folks lived longer in these parts when they lacked curiosity.

Yet seeing guards atop the towers, aiming their Winchesters and Gatling guns down at anyone daring enough to venture toward the private home, had never sat well with Dobie. He eased back on his

leathers and slowed his mount to a trot. Slim Baker
followed suit and looked at his superior. Unlike
Dobie, the deputy had never ridden to this place
before.

'What d'we slow up for, Sheriff?' the youngster
asked.

'To give them guards the chance to recognize us,
boy,' Dobie squinted through the eerie darkness at
the guard towers and then pulled back his top coat
so that his tin star caught the moon and starlight.
'We don't want them to accidentally shoot us, do we?'

Deputy Baker felt the spittle in his mouth dry up
and refuse to trail down his throat. His eyes darted
between the veteran lawman and the dark wall that
loomed over them. Then he noticed Dobie peel back
his top coat to expose the tin star pinned to his
leather vest.

'Show your star, boy,' the sheriff advised.

Baker looked confused. 'What for? We know who
we are.'

'But do them boys on them towers know?' Dobie
said as he steadied his horse and started to ride up
the trail toward the towering gates. 'If they see our
tin stars, they might not shoot.'

The deputy was horrified.

'Are you telling me that them varmints might
shoot us, Sheriff?' he croaked nervously. 'That ain't
exactly legal, is it?'

'Jeb James is the law in these parts, Slim,' Dobie
replied drily. 'Them guards are there to protect his
sorrowful hide and they'll kill anyone that they think

might pose a threat.'

Slim Baker gripped his reins tightly as the pair of saddle horses trotted to the gate post. He was trembling as their mounts came to a halt before the large gates. The sound of rifles being cocked and readied above them drew their attention to the men who loomed ominously above them.

Dobie studied the two Gatling guns gleaming in the light of stars and new moon. Both were aimed at them from the towers to either side of the gates. He had never seen the weapons before, but knew how lethal they could be in the right hands.

One of the men above them leaned over the wall and stared down at the pair of two riders. The heavenly light danced on the tin stars pinned to the lawmen's chests and dazzled like impish sprites.

'Is that you, Sheriff?' the sentry called out. 'This is a mighty strange time to come calling.'

Dobie nodded. 'I know it is, but it's important.'

The deputy was terrified as he sat beside the sheriff. He gripped his reins tightly and wished that he had not been ordered to accompany Dobie. He wanted to turn his mount around and spur away from this place, but remained. It might have been pride that prevented him from showing his true colours, but it felt more like stupidity. He was too damn scared to do anything apart from remain close to his superior.

'Open up these gates, sonny,' the sheriff boldly demanded as he leaned back on his saddle and stared up into the eerie darkness. 'I've got urgent information to tell Jeb.'

'It's late,' another voice piped up from the opposite side of the gate. 'Mr James is probably bedded down for the night, Sheriff. He ain't partial to being woke up.'

The sheriff extracted his silver pocket watch from his shirt front and flicked open its engraved lid. There was just enough moonlight to reveal the times to his wrinkled eyes.

'It ain't that late, sonny,' Dobie argued before returning the watch to his pocket. 'Jeb's still awake. So open up them gates before I die of old age.'

He could hear mumbling between a couple of the guards as they discussed whether they should or should not allow the lawmen to enter the compound.

After what seemed like an eternity, Dobie lost his temper and shook his fist at the shadowy figures angrily. 'Open up these damn gates and let us into the compound. Jeb will want to hear what we gotta tell him.'

After a few moments more the guards reluctantly agreed and called down to some of their fellow sentries to open the huge wooden gates.

The sound of activity filled both lawmen's ears as they waited for the gates to part.

'Maybe I should wait out here, Sheriff,' Baker whispered across the gap between their horses.

'You're coming with me, Slim,' Dobie said through gritted teeth, 'and I'm headed inside there to have me a confab with Jeb.'

The deputy shrugged in compliance. He was far

more scared of the sheriff than he was of the deadly weaponry that was aimed at them from the towers.

The gates slowly parted and moved inward revealing the shadowy interior between the wall and the house. The lawmen rode on through toward the moonlit house. The deputy kept glancing around them at the numerous men who roamed around the area between the large structure and the wall.

'What in tarnation does Mr James want with all these men guarding him, Sheriff?' he asked. 'I don't understand any of this.'

'Me neither,' Dobie admitted.

'Huh?' Baker's jaw dropped when he heard the admission.

'It's better that way, Slim,' Dobie said as they neared the hitching pole outside the large white-washed structure. The sheriff reined in and then looped his leg over the saddle cantle and dismounted. He secured his leathers and then looked up at the nervous deputy. 'The less we know, the safer we are.'

Baker scratched his neck. 'I just don't understand why anyone would need so much protection, Sheriff.'

The sheriff sighed heavily. 'Quit thinking about it. You might just live a tad longer if you stop trying to figure things out, Slim.'

Slim Baker knew he had been warned not to question things that had nothing to do with him. The reclusive James had his reasons and that was that. He nodded at his superior.

'Stay there,' Dobie ordered and turned before heading toward the black front door. The ground outside the grand house was covered with imported Mexican floor tiles. Even in the darkness they acted like mirrors.

Dobie ambled to an impressive large brass door knocker hanging like a metal bird of prey upon the door's black wooden surface. The sheriff reached up and was about to grab hold of the knocker when the door was suddenly opened.

Light from inside the structure cascaded over the lawman and temporarily blinded him.

SEVEN

The deep baritone voice that greeted Dobie was familiar and powerful as it halted the lawman in his tracks. The sheriff lowered his arm as his eyes slowly adjusted to the brilliantly lit hall. Gradually, he focused on the impressive stature of Jeb James standing before him.

'What the hell do you want, Dobie?' James boomed. 'Ain't you got a bed to go to?'

'It ain't that late, Jeb,' the sheriff blinked and then stepped into the house. Jeb James was a man in his late fifties but still stood close to six feet in height. Age had not weathered him as it tended to do to so many others in these parts. He closed the door and stared at the seasoned lawman before leading him into a room filled with books.

'You always were a damn night owl, Dobie,' James laughed and rested his hands on a drinks cabinet covered with numerous liquor bottles and a variety of fine glasses.

The sheriff moved closer to the large figure.

'I came here to tell you that there's a critter in town named Fire Wolf, Jeb,' Dobie explained as a glass of whiskey was thrust into his hand.

James frowned and then filled another glass with more of the strong liquor before moving to a heavily padded leather chair set close to a roaring log fire. The big man sat down and nursed the whiskey as the sheriff cautiously followed him like a faithful hound.

'Why are you telling me about some varmint named Fire Wolf, Dobie?' James asked as he sipped his whiskey. 'Who the hell is he? I've never heard of him.'

The statement troubled the lawman. He rested a hand on the stone fire surround and shook his head thoughtfully before returning his attention to James.

'So you didn't send for this Fire Wolf varmint, Jeb?' he checked. 'He told a bartender that you had sent for him. He wanted to know where you were but the lad played dumb and said he didn't know.'

The expression on James' face was thoughtful as he absorbed the words of the lawman. He shook his head. 'I've never even heard of him. Why would I send for anyone? I've got enough guards around here to fend off the Mexican army.'

Dobie drained his glass of the expensive whiskey and then placed the hand-crafted cut glass tumbler down. He rubbed his face and bit his lip as a million thoughts flashed through his mind.

'He's a deadly hired killer, Jeb,' the sheriff explained to the wealthy man. 'They reckon that he's

73

the most dangerous of his breed.'

'Why would I need someone like that, Dobie?' James took another sip of his whiskey. 'Every one of my boys out there is a killer. I sure don't need another one.'

Dobie moved to the lace drapes and stared out of the room's solitary window for a few moments. 'Then Fire Wolf was lured here by someone pretending to be you. He thinks that you sent for him and the varmint will be expecting a payday.'

'I sure ain't gonna pay him, Dobie,' James announced.

The sheriff was worried. He knew that if someone like Fire Wolf did not get his expected blood money, he might decide to take his anger out on the settlement itself.

'I've heard a few things about Fire Wolf over the years, Jeb,' he said. 'None of them are good. I sure don't wanna be facing that varmint if he's riled.'

James eased himself out of his chair and rested a hand on the back rest as he finished his whiskey. His eyes tightened as they watched the troubled lawman.

'Why are you so fired up about this Fire Wolf critter?' he asked. 'We've had drifters in Jamesburg before. You've handled them all. What's so different about this bastard?'

'He's a deadly killer,' Dobie said bluntly. 'I've heard that he'll kill anyone who either gets in his way or he's been paid to execute. Fire Wolf don't take prisoners. All he does is kill.'

James considered the lawman's words.

The sheriff turned and looked across the room at the man who practically owned the entire town of Jamesburg. He walked toward the tall man.

'If Fire Wolf ain't here to kill someone for you then I reckon he's here to kill you, Jeb,' Dobie said bluntly. 'There ain't no other option. That bastard only does one thing and that's killing and they say that there ain't anyone around that does it better.'

The expression on Jeb James' face went from slightly amused to slightly troubled. He moved back to where he had his stock of expensive alcohol was stored and poured himself another whiskey. This time he filled his glass to the brim. Dobie stood a few feet behind the big man.

'How'd he get his instructions, Dobie?'

'That I don't know, but I'd say it was by telegraph,' the lawman reasoned. 'Ain't nothing more impersonal that a wire. Anyone can sign any name they want to a telegraph.'

'You're right,' James agreed as he took a mouthful of the whiskey and then sighed. 'Someone in Jamesburg wants me dead and they're willing to pay a hired gunman to do it.'

'I thought you'd like to know,' Dobie started to walk back toward the hall.

'Dobie,' James said gruffly.

The veteran sheriff stopped and glanced at the troubled figure. His head tilted as he watched James stare into his whiskey tumbler.

'What, Jeb?' he asked.

'Kill this Fire Wolf critter and I'll give you a

thousand bucks,' James said without looking at the lawman. 'I don't care how you do it but kill him before he kills me.'

Dobie nodded.

'What about the varmint that intends hiring him to kill you, Jeb?' he asked. 'Do you want me to kill him as well or do you just want his name?'

Jeb James took a large swallow of the expensive whiskey and allowed its fiery contents to burn its way down into his innards as he considered the sheriff's question. He began to nod when the answer came to him.

Finally, James turned and looked at the lawman. A smile made its way across his hardened features and did not stop until it filled his entire face.

'You don't have to kill the man who wants me dead, old friend,' he grinned. 'Just tell me his name and my boys will do the rest. Nice and slow like the old days.'

Sheriff Dobie touched his hat brim. 'Understood.'

EIGHT

The moon and stars still cast their eerie light across the vast territory, but few within the remote settlement noticed anything apart from the scent of stale liquor and cheap perfume that dominated the heart of Jamesburg. The numerous cowboys who had congregated in the large town had no desire to look heavenward for their pleasures. The many saloons and whore houses provided everything they wanted within the lantern-lit town.

Men in various stages of drunkenness roamed from pleasure palaces to drinking holes. Only unconsciousness or empty pockets could stop them. The town might have still been quite busy yet few noticed the arrival of a man atop a muscular black gelding as he slowly entered the outskirts of Jamesburg.

Even if any of the locals had cast their attention in his direction, they would not have able to identify him. The horseman had a Mexican blanket draped over his hunched shoulders and wore a wide brimmed sombrero that hid his features from scrutiny.

There was no way that any prying eyes could get a clear picture of the mysterious rider who steered his elegant horse deeper into the sprawling settlement. As the horse walked down the centre of the main thoroughfare, he drew no attention from any of the drunken men that staggered from one building to the next.

That suited the heavily disguised rider just fine. He had no intension of being noticed as he entered the busiest part of the noisy town. He lifted his head and glanced out from under the large brim of his hat at the various menfolk wondering around aimlessly.

Then something caught his keen attention. It was the magnificent grey stallion tethered outside the Buckweed saloon beside a couple of far smaller saddle horses.

The horseman eased back on his decorated leathers and stopped the black gelding behind the high-shouldered stallion for a few moments. He studied the animal carefully. By the look of the stallion, it had ridden a long way and lathered-up sweat still clung to its chest.

The rider of the muscular black horse teased his reins to his left and then tapped his spurs into the animal's flanks. The gelding responded and started to walk on. The horse's master turned and continued to look at the stallion.

He knew most of the horses in these parts by sight. The grey stallion was not from any of the surrounding ranches. He was sure of that.

Could that horse belong to the hired killer that he had sent for using the name of the wealthiest man in Jamesburg? he asked himself. He returned his attention to what lay before him. He began to nod as his fertile imagination told him that he was correct.

That was Fire Wolf's horse.

He was sure of it.

That meant the notorious killer was somewhere within the boundaries of the boisterous town. All he had to do was find him and pay him his blood-money.

It sounded a lot simpler than it actually was though, and the horseman was only too aware of who he was dealing with. Fire Wolf was unlike any other gunman, and was known to have a vicious temper and be unpredictable. A troubling thought kept nagging at the rider's mind as the tall black horse continued to move through the lantern light.

What if Fire Wolf did not like being lured to a town by a lie? What if he turned his legendary wrath on his paymaster instead of his target?

An icy chill crept over the rider. It was like being stroked by the fingers of the Grim Reaper in readiness for his own demise.

He slowly raised his head and peered out from beneath the wide sombrero again. His eyes darted around the wide expanse before him as though in search of trouble. The main street was still busy but getting gradually quieter as night pressed on toward the inevitable coming of dawn.

The horseman tapped his spurs gently into the sides of the large black animal again and again. He suddenly realized that if Fire Wolf was already in town, he might be getting ready to meet with the reclusive Jeb James.

That might prove disastrous, he reasoned.

James and his small army of henchmen might shoot first and put a halt to his plan before it had even started. The gelding slowed by a stout tree set in the middle of the main street and the rider rested a hand upon its trunk. The horseman was anxious to find Fire Wolf before the hired killer found Jeb James.

Fire Wolf would have naturally thought that it was James who had sent for him and be more than a little angry when he discovered the truth. Fire Wolf would turn his guns on the man who had hired him and kill him without a second thought.

The horseman dismounted and wrapped his colourful reins around the tree trunk before securing them. He kept his blanket around his shoulders and then headed toward the only hotel in town.

The Gala hotel was not as grand as it sounded. It had roughly twelve rooms and had never in its history been more than half full. He stepped up on the boardwalk and reached out for the door handle. He entered the lobby and stared at the youngster behind the desk.

The young man who had his hair oiled but still looked little more that fifteen years of age looked up from behind the desk and watched the figure walking straight at him.

'I ain't allowed to rent rooms to Mexicans,' he piped up as the figure stopped by the desk.

'I ain't here for a room,' the voice from under the sombrero said as his hands turned the register around so that he could read the names written upon its pages.

'You don't sound like a Mexican,' the boy said curiously.

'I ain't Mexican,' the voice corrected gruffly. 'Are these the only folks you got staying here, boy?'

'They're the only folks we got staying here,' the youngster replied as he vainly attempted to look under the brim of the floppy sombrero. 'Why? And how come you're dressed up like a Mexican?'

The man beneath the sombrero turned and marched to the door at pace. He stepped back out on to the street and paused for a few moments as he closed the door behind his wide back.

'He must be in the Buckweed,' he muttered to himself before stepping down on to the moonlit sand and walking back to his horse. He grabbed the tail of his long leathers and tugged it free. The horseman grabbed his saddle horn and stepped back into his stirrup. He swung his right leg over the black and thrust it into the stirrup and turned the horse.

The horseman knew that he would have to find a place which gave him an uninterrupted view of the saloon if he were to be able to identify Fire Wolf when he appeared.

He kicked the horse into action. The gelding

trotted down the street which it had just travelled along. He slowed the animal down as he neared the brightly-lit Buckweed and then turned into an alley opposite the busy saloon.

The horseman stopped and turned the black horse until he was able to have an uninterrupted view of the saloon. The alley was bathed in darkness and provided good cover for the mysterious rider but he was still troubled.

He rested his hands on the saddle horn and stared out into the bright street. He wondered what the notorious Fire Wolf was really like and if he bore any resemblance to his deadly reputation.

Some men's legends grow far larger than the men themselves. Even so, Fire Wolf had to be one of the most lethal living creatures ever to have roamed the west, the horseman feared. No man had ever gained such a fearsome reputation without actually being pure evil.

The horseman swallowed hard. He remained under his makeshift disguise knowing that it was the only protection he had against being recognized by any of Jeb James' men.

He pulled the sombrero brim down and stared straight ahead at the Buckweed and watched men moving in and out of the busy saloon. His guts were a turmoil of anxiety. Part of him wanted Fire Wolf to show himself and the other feared meeting what most regarded as the most lethal man to ever take a breath.

Terror flowed through his every sinew as he sat

astride the black gelding and waited for Fire Wolf to step out from the saloon. Then his attention was drawn to a pair of drunken cowboys who were approaching the saloon. They were loud and both brandishing long-bladed knives.

'Oh hell,' he whispered to himself as he gripped his reins tightly. 'This ain't gonna turn out good if Fire Wolf makes an appearance.'

NINE

The distinctive sound of the pair of drunken cowhands filled the small bedroom above the saloon door and caused the tall figure to glance at the window drapes. Fire Wolf removed the bottle from the bargirl's hands and watched her snoring on the soft bed. He had never had any intention of doing anything except retrieve his whiskey bottle after trailing Mary Scott from the bar room to her bedroom. The noisy cowboys out in the street drew his attention as he lifted the bottle to his lips and took a long swallow. As he lowered the half empty vessel from his mouth, the noise from the street grew louder. So loud that it smothered all the saloon's other noises. Fire Wolf gave a grunt and then returned to the bedroom window as the fiery liquid trailed down his throat.

Fire Wolf could watch men, women or even children getting hurt or even killed with emotionless disdain but if anyone dared get close to his trusty mount, he got angry. So angry that he would think

84

nothing of killing.

He pulled the drape aside and stared down into the well-lit street. Then he noticed the pair of cowboys and the flashing blades of their knives. For a moment he did not react, but then he saw them staggering toward his grey stallion. An inferno in his innards ignited a fury deep inside him.

He had witnessed many so-called men in his time and learned that a handful of them took sickening pleasure in tormenting and even killing defenceless animals. The cowboys were drunkenly lashing out at one another with their knives as they neared his tethered high-shouldered grey stallion.

Fire Wolf had no doubt what they actually intended doing to his magnificent thoroughbred horse and it was not pretty. He snorted through flared nostrils and placed the bottle down on the small dresser next to the bed.

He then flicked the lock on the sash window and pulled it up. The evening fresh air hit the hired killer full on as his bony hand retrieved his hat and placed it on his mane of black hair. Silently he pushed his long left leg out through the open window and stepped on to the wooden shingles. Fire Wolf straightened up to his full height and then pushed the tails of his trail coat over his holstered .45s.

Although the cowboys did not realize it, they were dicing with death. Fire Wolf's calculating eyes burned down through the artificial light at the drunken men who had already reached his prized horse. The grey stallion snorted as the cowboys swung and jabbed their lethal stilettos in carefree abandon. They were jabbing out at one another, using the horse as a living shield between them.

Fire Wolf had seen enough. He walked down the incline to the very rim of the porch overhang and stared down at the men beneath him. They were now to either side of his snorting grey as the defenceless animal strained to break free of its restraints.

His hands drew his guns and cocked their hammers. The sound of the six-shooters being readied caught the liquor-sodden cowboys' attention. They momentarily stopped their dangerous antics and looked around the street at the dwindling crowds who were still moving to and from the other saloons.

The expression on their faces grew confused.

'Did you hear guns being cocked, Hank?' one of the cowboys asked his pal.

'I could have sworn I heard something, Bob,' the other cowboy answered as they continued to push the wide-eyed stallion hard until they were able to join forces alongside the water trough beside the hitching pole.

The first cowboy swung on his heels and waved his knife at the tall horse. 'I'm gonna skin that critter, Hank. I'm gonna make him as ugly as the rest of the horses in Jamesburg.'

'Do it, Bob,' his pal encouraged. 'I'm sick of these rich dudes and their pretty horses cluttering up town. We work our tails off and we can't afford anything as pretty as that. Stick him. Stick him good.'

Both cowboys roared with laughter as they made their way back to the skittish stallion.

'I wouldn't do that if I was you,' Fire Wolf sounded almost as angry as he actually was.

The staggering men looked up at the porch roof and saw the unearthly sight as he toyed with his cocked six-shooters. They pointed at the man in black with their knives and continued laughing.

'Look at that critter, Hank,' the grinning cowboy pointed with his knife. 'That dude thinks he can scare real cowboys. Look at him, for Pete's sake. He's so clean it's pitiful.'

Fire Wolf squeezed both his triggers.

The sound of the deafening shots bounced off the sturdy structures as dust kicked up the sand between both cowboys. The men were not impressed.

'Get down here, boy,' the cowboy screamed out at Fire Wolf as the deadly killer cocked his guns again. 'Me and Bob don't scare as easy as stinking clean varmints. We're real men and we don't listen to cotton-picking dudes like you.'

The cowboys patted each other on the back, continued laughing and then proceeded on their way back to the high-shouldered stallion.

'I'm gonna stick my knife so deep into this nag he'll be spitting blood,' the cowboy bragged.

'I'm gonna geld this critter, Hank,' the other laughed as he wandered toward the back of the stallion and attempted to grab hold of the animal's tail. 'You listen to this nag squeal when I start cutting.'

The man in black grew even angrier. He knew that

he would have to act soon if his precious mount were not to get itself skinned or worse.

Fire Wolf strode along the wooden shingles until he was balanced on the very edge of the porch and directly above his defenceless horse. Just as he had silently predicted, the drunken men had done what so many mindless creatures tended to do and had already hurt the handsome horse.

He moved his hands constantly and kept the cowboys in his sights. Then he watched in horror as the closest cowboy jabbed out with his knife and caught the stallion in the shoulder.

The street echoed to the hideous sound of the stallion as the animal felt the long knife blade cut into its flesh. The stallion kicked out desperately and bucked as it struggled with the taut reins holding it in check by the hitching pole.

Fire Wolf had seen enough. His fury exploded as he raised his left, levelled the .45 and squeezed its trigger.

He watched as his bullet shattered the cowboy's hand sending the knife flying into the air alongside fingers and lumps of gore. The air was filled with crimson droplets of blood. Then his eyes darted to the other cowboy who stood close to the rear of the grey.

The sight of his pal losing half of his hand shook the drunken cowboy to the core. He dropped his dagger and stared up at the grim-faced Fire Wolf as the emotionless hired executioner aimed the weapon in his right hand straight at him.

'Don't shoot,' he begged waving his hands frantically as his badly injured pal gripped his wrist in a vain attempt to stop blood from pouring out of his hand. 'Please don't shoot.'

The begging had no effect on Fire Wolf.

He trained his gun at the pleading man and then pulled back on its trigger. A flash of bright light exploded from the .45 as a cloud of gunsmoke encircled the weapon.

The wounded cowboy looked in horror as the bullet hit his pal between the eyes sending him spinning on his boots before crashing into the sand behind him. The badly injured cowboy staggered away from his lifeless cohort as he watched Fire Wolf cock both his smoking guns again.

The cowboy fell on to his knees and looked up at the unsmiling face of the gunman. He screamed out in a pointless bid for mercy.

'Don't kill me,' the cowboy pleaded as he watched the tall figure jump down to the street. Dust kicked up around the boots of the man in black as he steadied himself and glared at the kneeling cowboy. 'I beg you. Don't kill me. Me and Hank was just having a few laughs.'

Fire Wolf started to walk toward the injured cowboy with his smoking .45s gripped in his hands. When he was directly above the cowboy, he paused.

His stony stare glanced at his mount and saw the blood staining the stallion's shoulder as it trickled from the stab wound. He returned to the cowboy and shook his head.

'This ain't your lucky day,' he quietly drawled.

Fire Wolf levelled his six-shooters at the kneeling cowboy and strode straight up to the sobbing man. He pressed the cold steel barrels into the face of the cowboy and then spat. The spittle ran down the cowboy's face as he looked up at the fearsome Fire Wolf above him.

'Please,' the cowboy began to rant repeatedly.

Fire Wolf shook his head and then pulled back on the triggers of both his weapons. The cowboy's head exploded into a sickening crimson mess as the bullets shattered his skull.

The emotionless man in black watched as the limp body crumpled on to the sand before him. He spat again at what was left of the cowboy and then holstered his guns and turned toward his injured horse.

Fire Wolf stared at the hideous wound as blood continued to flow from the animal. He pulled the long leathers free of the hitching pole and then led the tall animal around the bodies as blood slowly surrounded them.

'They'll be stiff as soon as the sun rises, Ghost,' Fire Wolf said in a deep voice as he gathered up the reins and steadied the injured stallion. 'I gotta find a livery stable and get you fixed up.'

The tall man in black was about to raise his left leg and push its boot into his stirrup when he sensed he was being watched. Fire Wolf glanced over the saddle with narrowed eyes and studied the drunken folks who were still staggering around the street totally unaware of what had just occurred.

Seeing nothing to alarm him, Fire Wolf grabbed the stallion's mane and quickly mounted. He gathered up the reins and carefully turned the injured animal and tapped his spurs.

'Come on, Ghost,' he urged.

The injured thoroughbred walked slowly along the main street as its master searched for a livery stable where he might locate someone who could tend to his mount. Fire Wolf sniffed at the night air. He knew that wherever the livery stable might be situated, his nose would find it long before his eyes.

'Keep going, horse,' he growled.

With each step of the animal's long legs, Fire Wolf noticed blood squirting from the knife wound. He gritted his teeth and kept encouraging the stallion on.

Fire Wolf knew that he might have dispatched the cowboys to Boot Hill easily, but wondered how badly injured his faithful mount actually was. He had already stayed in Jamesburg far longer than he had planned and if the stallion was badly hurt, he might be forced to remain here even longer.

That troubled Fire Wolf.

The longer anyone in his chosen profession was forced to remain in one place, the greater the danger was for them. Men with Fire Wolf's notorious reputation would attract every hopeful gunman within a hundred miles.

Fire Wolf had no desire to befall that fate.

There was no financial gain in that.

Yet the deadly man in black would not leave

without his prized grey stallion. It had taken years for him to find a horse as loyal as this one and he would not cut and run.

The puzzling thought of Jeb James filled the deadly mind as he continued searching for a livery stable. Who exactly was this character and why had he sent for the lethal assassin?

Doubts began to fill his mind.

Fire Wolf wondered if he had actually been duped into travelling to this remote settlement for someone's ulterior purpose. As the injured grey slowly meandered through the side streets, its master reloaded his guns with fresh ammunition from his gun belt.

This was getting damn complicated, he thought. Fire Wolf hated complications. There was usually no profit in them.

TEN

As Fire Wolf reached the outskirts of town, he noticed that the stallion was limping badly. He swiftly dismounted beneath a street lantern and checked the horse carefully for other injuries before looking at the knife wound again. The street lantern's amber light made it quite obvious that the animal was far more severely injured than he had at first assumed. Fire Wolf stared at the horse. Blood stained the entire leg from the shoulder to its hoof.

He sighed heavily and then noticed the tall livery stable less than fifty feet from where he was standing. He patted the horse's neck and picked up its reins.

'Come on, Ghost,' he said. 'We'd better get this fixed up as fast we can.'

Fire Wolf slowly walked the limping stallion toward the fragrant structure. With each step he scanned the surrounding area for any signs of trouble. Fire Wolf sniffed the air and then observed the glowing light coming from within its heart.

'Maybe we can get you sewn up in there, Ghost,'

he told the horse as he neared the massive wooden structure. The grey stallion followed its master through the open barn doors into the heart of the tall building. Fire Wolf stopped as the heat of the forge welcomed them. He glanced around the large area and noticed several horses in stalls at the back end of the stable.

'Howdy, stranger,' a gruff voice came from a corner as a well-built man walked from the shadows toward them. The man looked as though he would be able to snap a tree with his eyelids as he closed in on the hired killer and the blood-soaked stallion.

Fire Wolf glanced at the blacksmith as the burly man walked around the tall grey before returning to the obvious stab wound.

'My horse got on the bad side of a couple of drunks with knives,' the man in black informed the blacksmith. 'Can you tend his wound?'

The man placed a large paw on the neck of the grey, wiped the blood off the animal's shoulder and stared at the wound carefully. 'This is a real bad wound, stranger.'

Fire Wolf dropped the reins.

'Can you fix him?' he asked. 'Can you?'

The blacksmith nodded. 'Sure, but you can't ride him for at least a week. We gotta let his wound knit together. It'll take time and a good portion of luck.'

'I'll leave him here with you,' Fire Wolf said before pulling out a golden eagle and handing it to the blacksmith. 'Will this cover it?'

A wry smile etched the large man's face. He tested

the coin with his teeth and then nodded.

'What's the name?' he asked.

'I call him Ghost,' the man in black replied.

'I meant your name, stranger,' the blacksmith grinned.

'Fire Wolf,' he said.

The blacksmith looked the tall figure up and down and then nodded. He smiled and then smacked his hands together as he started to remove the horse's saddle.

'My name's Tor,' he said as he hooked the fender on the saddle horn and began to release the cinch strap. 'Nice to meet you, Fire Wolf. I've heard about you.'

Fire Wolf cleared his throat.

'You have?'

Tor smiled as he dragged the saddle off the back of the grey and carefully placed it on a stall wall. The muscular blacksmith grabbed a copper bucket, scooped water out of a barrel and placed it on the hot coals of his forge. His knowing eyes looked at the man in black.

'Well?' he asked as his powerful right arm pumped the bellows and caused the coals to redden. Sparks floated up from the glowing coals and vanished into a large extraction chimney that hung over the forge. 'Any of those tales of you killing folks for handsome money happen to be true?'

Without a moment's hesitation Fire Wolf fired a reply straight back at the curious blacksmith.

'Most of it,' Fire Wolf nodded as he pulled out a

cigar from his jacket pocket and bit off its tip. He spat at the straw-littered ground and then concentrated his eagle-like attention at the wide open barn doors and the darkness beyond.

Tor Olsen noticed that Fire Wolf seemed unable to drag his eyes from the shadowy street as his long fingers searched for a match in his vest pockets.

'What you looking at?' he asked as he continued to pump the bellows. 'There ain't nothing out there to trouble us.'

Fire Wolf shook his head.

'I'm not troubled, Tor,' he muttered as his teeth gripped the cigar. 'There is somebody out there though.'

'Yeah?' The large man leaned away from the intense heat and also looked out to the street. 'I don't see nothing.'

'Me neither, but I've heard him for the last ten minutes or so,' Fire Wolf said as he lifted a match and pressed his thumbnail against its colourful tip. 'He trailed me just after I dealt with those knife-wielding cowpokes.'

Tor exhaled loudly. 'You must have mighty good hearing.'

Fire Wolf nodded in agreement and then returned his full attention to the eerily lit street.

The large sweating figure knew that it was dangerous to risk riling a man like Fire Wolf, but could not control his morbid curiosity.

'You here to do some killing?' the blacksmith wondered.

'I already done some killing, Tor,' Fire Wolf informed as he struck a match and raised its flame to the tip of the cigar and inhaled the smoke. 'Those knife-carrying cowpokes I told you about. I already killed them. Nobody hurts Ghost and lives to brag about it.'

The chilling words washed over the blacksmith as he continued to work the bellows. Yet even though he could almost taste the danger standing a few feet from him, he was still curious.

'Are you here to kill anybody in particular besides those dumb bastards, Fire Wolf?' he asked.

Fire Wolf scratched the side of his nose with his thumbnail and nodded. 'A critter named Jeb James sent me a telegraph, but I ain't located him yet.'

The expression on the larger man's creased face altered. He stopped his actions and walked back to the horse and checked the wound again before turning and looking at the emotionless face of the hired killer.

'Do you know who Jeb James is, Fire Wolf?' he asked.

'A bartender told me that he practically owns this town,' Fire Wolf answered. 'Apart from that, I've never even heard of him before.'

Tor straightened up and rubbed the sweat off his face. He looked concerned by his newly found friend's ignorance. He strode back to the man in black and saw the ivory gun grips hidden beneath the long trail coat.

'James is the richest varmint in the territory, Fire

97

Wolf,' he explained. 'He's got himself an army and lives in a house behind a huge stone wall. Folks around here call it a fort. It sure looks like a fort. Anybody might think he's expecting an attack by Injuns but there ain't bin any Injuns around here in twenty years.'

Thoughtfully, Fire Wolf inhaled again until his lungs were filled with the toxic cigar smoke. After allowing the smoke to linger for a while he then exhaled. The smoke slowly filtered through his teeth.

'Jeb James must be very frightened,' he reasoned.

Tor Olsen raised his eyebrows in surprise by the statement and drew closer to the last of the Mandan. A pained expression etched his whiskered face.

'Frightened?' he repeated.

Fire Wolf nodded. 'Why else would he hide in a fortress with a small army guarding him, Tor? Only fear makes a man act like that.'

'I always figured he must have himself something real valuable in there,' the blacksmith said. 'Maybe gold or maybe he discovered pirate treasure. That galoot sure is rich and nobody has ever figured out how he managed to get so rich.'

'Maybe,' the man in black sighed.

'It has to be treasure of some kind,' Tor insisted.

'I still say Jeb James sounds fearful,' Fire Wolf stared through his cigar smoke into the dark street and then gently eased the blacksmith away from him. His left hand then dropped until its palm rested on the holstered gun grip. His fingers curled around the deadly weapon as he stepped toward the massive entrance.

The blacksmith could tell that something out in the darkness had caught the attention of the infamous killer. Fire Wolf moved stealthily toward the towering barn doors. He silently stared out into the moonlight and focused hard.

'What's wrong?' Tor asked as he ran a large hand along the neck of the grey stallion. 'What you seen?'

Fire Wolf did not reply as he continued to the barn doors and rested his wide back against one of them. His cold eyes searched the shadows like a cougar waiting for its chosen prey to betray itself.

Every instinctive sense in his long lean body tingled as he chewed on the cigar thoughtfully. He knew that the man he sought was out there somewhere.

Somewhere close.

Many men had tried to kill Fire Wolf over the years and he was not about to allow it to happen again. His finger curled around the trigger of the holstered gun on his left hip.

'What the hell's wrong, Fire Wolf?' Tor Olsen asked the last of the Mandan.

Fire Wolf stepped away from the wide doors and raised his right hand in a gesture to mute the burly blacksmith. Tor fell silent and watched the deadly assassin in awe. He knew that Fire Wolf was defiantly making himself a target and that took courage. A whole heap of courage.

Fire Wolf stopped walking when he was exactly

between the tall barn doors. He turned slightly and positioned himself at an angle to where he was looking. If anyone was foolhardy enough to take a shot at him, he reasoned, he would prove a difficult target. Fire Wolf filled his lungs with cigar smoke and savoured it for a few seconds before exhaling.

'Show yourself,' he shouted through cigar smoke.

His raised voice must have scared his observer.

He suddenly caught sight of movement twenty feet from the barn doors. Faster than seemed humanly possible, Fire Wolf drew the six-shooter from its holster and cocked its hammer. His eyes narrowed and honed in on his target.

Fire Wolf fired.

ELEVEN

The sound of a man yelping like a whipped dog filled the surrounding area. Wooden splinters rose into the moonlight as a solitary bullet went through an upturned wagon and located its target. With smoke snaking from the barrel of his six-shooter, Fire Wolf cocked the gun's hammer again and approached the pitiful cries. His long legs strode across the ground to where he could hear the painful whimpering. His eyes focused on the upturned wagon and listened to what was hidden just behind its weathered flatbed.

The large hole in the wagon's planking smouldered from the heat of the bullet that Fire Wolf had just sent through it. His keen hearing knew exactly where the wounded man was hiding behind the rickety vehicle.

A morbid grin etched his otherwise emotionless features as he closed in on where he instinctively calculated his target was vainly attempting to secrete itself. Fire Wolf stopped a few feet away from the shadowy wagon.

He levelled the six-shooter and then kicked the tailgate so violently it was ripped from the weathered body of the wagon and flew across the sand.

'Crawl out or I'll surely kill you,' Fire Wolf snarled venomously. 'I've just about had my fill of this town and the loco-beans that live here.'

'Don't shoot, Fire Wolf,' a voice begged from behind the lumber. 'I don't mean you no misery.'

The man in black was uneasy.

'How d'you know my name?' he growled. 'I don't recall being introduced to no dust-crawling folks in this damn town.'

'I'll explain,' the voice grunted. Slowly he saw two hands appear in the ghostly moonlight as the wounded man crawled out from cover. The man had a blanket covering his shoulders and a sombrero hanging by its drawstring on his back. He stopped crawling and then cautiously glanced up at the fearsome Fire Wolf. 'I wasn't trying to back-shoot you or nothing. You gotta believe me.'

A lifetime of brutal slayings had taught Fire Wolf never to believe or blindly trust anyone. But his instinct to simply kill this excuse for a man was overwhelmed by his curiosity as how he knew his name.

'Get on your damn feet,' the lethal sharpshooter ordered.

With the groans that only a wounded man could muster, the man gradually managed to stand upright. He swayed on his boots as Fire Wolf looked him up and down. Fire Wolf's bullet had ripped the side of the stranger's shirt apart and taken a chunk out of the man's side. Even the eerie moonlight could not conceal the painful wound from the hired killer's eyes.

'What are you meant to be?' Fire Wolf asked as smoke filtered between his gritted teeth. 'You sure ain't no Mexican.'

The man inhaled and clutched his grazed side.

'I'm the critter that sent for you, Fire Wolf,' he bluntly stated.

Fire Wolf spat the cigar at the sand and looked puzzled. He sighed and then holstered his gun before turning and silently walking back toward the livery stable.

'Follow me,' he drawled.

The wounded man winced with every step as he trailed the man in black back into the large building. He watched as Fire Wolf reached the middle of the straw-covered floor and then suddenly spun on his heels to face him. He stopped walking and stared in terror at the fearsome figure before him.

Angrily, Fire Wolf raised an accusing finger and aimed it at the man who had drawn him to Jamesburg on false pretences.

'You sent me that wire?' he yelled.

The bleeding man held his side hard in a bid to stem the blood flow and sheepishly nodded at the furious hired killer.

'I'm afraid I did, Fire Wolf,' he stammered. 'I had to get you here and I didn't wanna use my own name.'

Fire Wolf was confused.

'Why?' he shouted whilst the blacksmith innocently moved closer to the injured stranger as if he was going to inspect the bullet graze. 'Get out of the way, Tor. I still might kill him and I don't want you standing between him and me. You gotta tend Ghost first.'

The burly blacksmith looked at Fire Wolf. 'But he's wounded, Fire Wolf. I was only gonna check to see if he needed sewing up.'

'Sew my horse up first, Tor,' Fire Wolf fumed as he continued to stare at the bleeding stranger. 'Not that lying bastard. I don't give a damn if he bleeds to death. His lying brought me halfway across the territory.'

Fire Wolf rested both his hands on his holstered gun grips and glared in fury across the livery stable. He studied the wounded man with cold calculation.

He was somewhere in his mid-twenties, with hair the colour of damp sand and blue eyes. Just as Fire Wolf had already said, he was no Mexican. It was difficult for the man in black to tell how tall he was as he kept buckling in pain. Finally, he gritted his teeth and looked straight at the last of the Mandan in youthful defiance.

'My name's Joel Majors,' he uttered.

Fire Wolf frowned.

'Frankly, I don't give a damn what your name is,' he raged and shook his fist at Majors. 'You lied to me. I've killed folks for lying to me, and I ought to kill you.'

Majors removed the sombrero and then shook the

blanket off his shoulders. Both landed on the straw-covered ground. He then glanced down at the blood trickling from between his fingers as his hand pressed into his grazed flesh. He summoned every scrap of his strength and looked at Fire Wolf.

'I had to get you here,' he sighed. 'You're the only critter that can do what we need doing.'

Fire Wolf took two steps closer to the youngster.

'And what exactly do you need doing?' he asked. 'I'm a killer, boy. That's all I do. I just kill. Nobody does it better but if you got some notion that I can sort out any other problems you might have, you're sadly wrong.'

Majors forced himself to straighten up.

'That's just what we need doing, Fire Wolf,' he nodded. 'We need a killer. You're said to be the best there is. We need your services.'

Fire Wolf was still unsure of the young man. He pulled out another thin cigar from his inside pocket and tore its tip off with his teeth. He spat the tobacco at the ground and then placed it in the corner of his mouth.

'I've lost a mighty big payday coz of you, Majors,' he growled before plucking a match from his pocket and striking it with his thumbnail. He touched the end of the cigar and filled his lungs with smoke before discarding the match on to the forge coals.

Majors shook his head. 'No you ain't, Fire Wolf. You ain't lost a red cent.'

Fire Wolf raised an eyebrow.

'What you mean?' he asked curiously.

105

Majors staggered forward and looked hard into the taller man's eyes.

'I'm here to hire your skills, Fire Wolf,' Majors said. 'And pay your fee in full.'

Fire Wolf watched as the blacksmith began to bathe the grey stallion's deep stab wound in warm water from the metal pail. He then turned his head and stared straight into the face of the nervous Majors.

'You know how much I charge for killing?' he asked as smoke filtered through his teeth.

Majors nodded and slid a hand inside his shirt.

'I know. I done my homework. If you'll check this envelope I think you'll find the right amount,' he said.

Fire Wolf watched as Majors pulled out a fat envelope and handed it to him. The infamous killer opened the envelope looked at the wad of bank notes. He then nodded and returned his attention to the youngster.

'Who do you want killed?'

TWELVE

The pair of lawmen had not said much to one another on their return from Jeb James' fortress. Dobie knew that his very existence as the appointed sheriff of Jamesburg had nothing to do with merit, but on his obeying his old friend's every whim.

At any time James could turn on the veteran lawman as he had done to many of Dobie's predecessors. Jeb James ruled the town he had established and built twenty years earlier like an ancient king.

His word was the law and nobody ever forgot that simple fact. The reclusive James could have anyone killed should they disobey him and Dobie was sure that he had done so many times in the past.

Upon arriving back in Jamesburg the sheriff and his deputy had discovered the bodies of the two cowboys. Upon inspection it was obvious that both men had not just died in a brawl but had been executed with sickening precision.

Yet nobody in Jamesburg had seen a thing.

The lawmen entered the small office and closed

107

the door behind them. They added a few logs to the belly of the stove and placed a fresh pot of coffee on the flat top.

Dobie was unusually quiet as he rested in his swivel chair behind his desk and stared into infinity as though searching for inspiration. He had been told what to do but it did not sit well with the lawman.

Slim Baker on the other hand had not stopped chattering since they had returned to town. Yet his words had fallen on deaf ears. Finally, he glanced at the sheriff, rubbed the sweat off his brow and stared at the brooding lawman.

He snapped his fingers a few times until he managed to get his superior's attention. The deputy shook his head and looked at the older man with bemused interest.

'What in tarnation is wrong, Sheriff?' he asked.

Dobie sighed and then pulled his elbows off the ink blotter and leaned back on his chair.

'Nothing's wrong, Slim,' he replied.

The younger lawman was not normally argumentative but he had worked alongside Dobie long enough to be able to sense when the older character had something gnawing at his craw.

'The hell there ain't,' he said picking up their tin cups and placing them next to the coffee pot. 'You ain't said a damn word since you came out of Jeb James' fancy house. You've bin like a turkey on the night before Thanksgiving. What the hell is wrong, Sheriff?'

Dobie smiled and tried to dismiss his actions.

'I've just had a long day and I ain't getting any younger, Slim,' he exhaled and tapped his pipe bowl on his desk until its burned contents fell on the edge of the stained wood.

Baker frowned and looked at Dobie as he refilled his pipe bowl with fresh tobacco from his pouch.

'That ain't it,' he argued with a snort. 'James said something to you and it must have bin mighty upsetting. You've just clammed up.'

Dobie pushed tobacco down into his pipe bowl with his thumb and then placed its stem between his teeth. He patted his vest, found a match and then scratched it across his tin star.

'You got a real imagination there, Slim,' he grinned as he sucked the flame down into his primed pipe and blew a cloud of aromatic smoke at his concerned junior. 'I'm just tuckered, that's all.'

Brown was still not convinced by the explanation but knew that was all he was going to get. He strode to the hat stand and plucked his top coat off one of its hooks and put it on. As he buttoned up the coat, he retrieved his Stetson and placed it over his thick mane of hair.

'I'm taking me walk around town, Sheriff,' he announced as he gripped the door knob and twisted it. 'The coffee will be ready by the time I get back here. I'll pour us some when I finish my rounds.'

Dobie pulled the pipe from his lips and leaned forward.

'Don't go looking for Fire Wolf, Slim,' he warned. 'It ain't healthy to rile a critter like him. Look what

109

happened to them cowpokes we found outside the Buckweed.'

Baker paused.

'Do you reckon it was that Fire Wolf varmint that killed them boys, Sheriff?' he drily asked the veteran lawman.

The sheriff gave a nod of his head.

'I can't think of anyone else that could or would put so many bullets in heads like them cowpunchers had done to them, boy,' he shrugged and started puffing on his pipe stem again until a cloud hung over him. 'If you see Fire Wolf, give him a wide berth. He might be a high priced killer but he also takes pleasure in killing for free.'

The deputy gave a slight chuckle.

'I ain't gonna get killed by nobody,' he said before opening the office door and stepping out into the lantern-lit night.

Dobie rubbed his colourless features with his hand as he chewed on the pipe stem. He watched the deputy walk past the office window and vanish from view.

The instructions that Jeb James had given him were weighing heavily on the lawman. All he had to do was kill the infamous Fire Wolf after he had discovered the identity of the man who wanted to hire him.

It sounded impossible.

Maybe it was, but the thought of earning a thousand bucks kept nagging at the sheriff. It hung like an irresistible carrot before him, making any rational thoughts vaporise in the lawman's mind.

With that much money he could retire and live

what was left of his life in comfort. He stared hard at the pot belly stove and the blackened coffee pot resting on its flat surface and sighed. Some things took a long time to boil, he thought.

Other things erupted into action far faster and tended to catch folks unawares.

The sheriff wondered what the infamous Fire Wolf intended and what his intentions with Jeb James actually were. His seasoned mind tried to figure out exactly what the deadly hired killer was doing in Jamesburg. Was he telling the truth about looking for Jeb James? Or was there something else about his arrival in the remote town that Fire Wolf was keeping to himself? Was James telling the truth that he had not sent for the most lethal gunman in the vast untamed territory or was he also lying? So many damn questions and not a single satisfying answer to any of them.

Sheriff Dobie thought about the order he had received from James. Most of the previous demands he had been given by the wealthy rancher had been easily brushed under the table, but the promise of a thousand dollars made this different.

All he had to do was kill Fire Wolf. The trouble with men like the last of the Mandan was that they did not die easily.

'Boil, damn it,' he snarled at the coffee pot before opening his desk drawer and pulling out an unopened half pint of whiskey and placing it on the stained ink blotter. He broke its seal and extracted its cork. 'On second thoughts, I need something far stronger if I'm ever gonna figure this out.'

111

THIRTEEN

The lights of Jamesburg sparkled in the night sky as the two horsemen reached the frost-covered range. They glanced up at the ridge, drew rein and studied the line of amber lights that marked where the ground ended and the vast star-filled heavens began.

Lane Holden leaned on his saddle horn and stared at the lights for a few moments as his partner took a swig of water from his canteen. He looked at Ben Allen and scratched his jawline.

'That,' he informed, 'is Jamesburg, my old friend. Don't think it's as small as them lights would leave you to believe. I've been here before and it's big. Real big.'

Allen screwed the stopper back on to his canteen and then hung it from the saddle horn. He dried his lips on his sleeve and then turned on his saddle to look at Holden.

'I ain't never heard of the damn place, Lane,' he said. 'How come such a big town is out here in the middle of nowhere?'

Holden leaned back against his cantle. 'It's all down to a critter called Jeb James. He built it and rules over the damn place like he was some kinda ancient king or the like.'

Allen rubbed his face. He was still angry that after less than an hours' sleep in the old saloon back at Gold Strike, Holden had decided to start tracking the mysterious gunman who had killed three of their gang.

'Why d'we have to start hunting that bastard before sunrise, Lane?' he grumbled before yawning. 'I had hardly started dreaming when you woke me up. How come? If it is that Fire Wolf varmint we're trailing, I sure ain't in any rush to find him.'

'I'll tell you exactly why I changed my mind and figured we should start tracking that galoot, Ben,' Holden placed a fresh cigar between his teeth and scratched a match with his thumbnail. He raised the cupped flame to the long cigar and sucked in its toxic smoke. 'I couldn't sleep back there. I kept thinking about that critter. I figured that if he was Fire Wolf like I think he is, we gotta act fast to stand any chance of getting our hands on the money he's going to get paid.'

'But I could have had a few hours more sleep, Lane,' Allen complained wearily. 'I don't see what the hurry is.'

Holden steadied his mount. 'I've heard that Fire Wolf works fast, Ben. He gets paid and then kills his target and then rides out as fast as spit. If we catch up with him during the hours of darkness we got a

113

chance of bushwhacking the varmint after he's bin paid.'

Allen yawned and shrugged. 'I'm too damn tuckered to argue with you, Lane. Can we carry on to Jamesburg so I can find me somewhere to sleep?'

Holden nodded and took his partner's long leathers.

'You get yourself some shuteye, Ben,' he said before tapping his spurs. 'I'll follow the trail and steer your horse on into Jamesburg and wake you up when we get there.'

They continued on toward the sparkling amber lights that fringed the ridge. Neither had any notion of what they were actually heading into.

FOURTEEN

The lantern-lit streets of Jamesburg were covered in a layer of sparkling frost as the night reached its zenith. There were still a few hours left before sun-up and the main thoroughfare was quieter than it had been earlier. More and more of the revellers made their way back to their homes as either exhaustion or empty pockets brought an end to their night's enjoyment.

A few of the more resilient cowboys from the outlying ranches still tried to milk every last moment of pleasure before they too had to concede that they were finally defeated.

Tinny pianos wailed out the last of their repetitive tunes and filled the ears of the remaining customers who were determined to savour every last drop of pleasure out of the night, but one man seemed oblivious to all of it.

His mind was filled with the bemusing information and happenings of the previous few hours. None of which made any sense to the young lawman.

As was his nightly habit, Deputy Slim Baker walked through the lantern-lit streets. Yet he had more on his mind than the drunken customers who staggered between the saloons and the ever-busy whore houses. Blood still covered the ground where he and Dobie had discovered the bodies of the cowboys when they had ridden back into the sprawling town.

Baker walked through the stained sand as he crossed the street toward the opposite boardwalk. Yet even with his boots bloodied the naïve deputy had something else gnawing at his fertile imagination. Something which he just could not understand.

It was the way Dobie had been acting since his meeting with the reclusive Jeb James. Baker wondered what James might have said to the sheriff and why Dobie was behaving the way he was since they had returned to town.

It was totally uncharacteristic of the veteran lawman and it troubled the deputy more than he would ever admit to himself as he continued on his rounds.

None of it made any sense.

In all the time that he had known the sheriff, Baker had never seen the man act the way he had been doing since they had left the massive fortress.

The street lanterns further away from the heart of Jamesburg no longer cast their orange hue across the wooden boardwalks and store fronts.

A third of the lanterns had gone out as they ran dry of coal tar oil. There was nothing unusual about that and Baker paid it no heed as he kept taking his normal route around the large settlement. Amber light from a handful of windows still burned behind their lace drapes and reflected off various porch roofs but Baker seemed oblivious to them as he neared a corner. This was the poorer part of Jamesburg where even lawmen thought twice about entering on their lonesome.

Dobie had told his deputy to avoid the area around the ramshackle buildings when he was alone. Folks in this part of town had no liking for the law and even less for men who wore tin stars, but none of that had ever worried Baker.

He had been raised in a far more dangerous section of Laramie and as far as he was concerned there was nothing that could compare to that.

The deputy paused and studied the array of differing structures. He pulled out his tobacco pouch and pulled a thin gummed paper from it with his teeth. He then calmly began to sprinkle fine tobacco on to the paper curled expertly around his fingers. When the paper was primed, he tightened the drawstring of the pouch with his teeth and returned it to his pocket. He then slid his tongue along the gummed edge of the paper and turned the cigarette with his fingers.

While his fingers completed the job of creating the small stick of tobacco, his fertile imagination continued to try and work out what was wrong with Dobie.

Baker licked the cigarette, then placed it between his lips as his eyes darted from one shadow to the

117

next. Satisfied that there was no danger, he located a match and cupped it in his fingers. He was about to strike the match when he noticed something he considered unusual at this hour in this particular part of Jamesburg. Baker took two steps and then stared across the waste ground beyond the buildings at the tall livery stable two hundred yards from where he stood. Lantern light cascaded from its wide open barn doors and flooded over the area in front of the large structure.

'That's mighty strange,' Baker mumbled.

At first glance the livery looked as though it were on fire as light danced around its vast interior and cascaded out on to the surrounding ground. Then Baker realized that it was simply the light of numerous lanterns and the glowing coals of its forge that he was observing.

It still appeared wrong though. He knew that Tor Olsen was not a man to waste coal tar oil for no reason. The deputy scratched his head thoughtfully.

Baker ran the match across his pants leg and cupped its flickering flame. He lifted it to the cigarette between his lips and sucked in smoke.

He was about to continue checking the store fronts, as was his nightly routine, when his curiosity got the better of him and forced him to return his attention back to the brightly illuminated livery stable.

'Now that's kinda strange,' the deputy muttered as smoke drifted from his mouth and he concentrated on the fragrant structure. 'Old Tor don't usually waste money on needless light at this hour. I wonder why he's burning so much oil?'

No matter how hard the deputy tried to dismiss his curiosity, it was impossible. Baker hated mysteries and always sought to figure them out as quickly as he could.

'Damn it all,' he cursed as he inhaled deeply on his cigarette and started toward the livery stable as though drawn like a moth to a naked flame. 'I'd best find out why old Tor has all his lanterns blazing at this time of the night. If I don't, I'll not get any sleep tonight.'

The deputy strayed off the main street and started to make his way across the rough ground to where the large building stood.

The closer the young lawman got to the fragrant structure, the more he could see. Baker slowed his pace and sucked the last of the smoke from his cigarette and then dropped it on to the sand as he neared the upturned wagon.

As he crushed the fragile butt under his boot heel, he saw something high-lighted by the lantern light that washed over the sand.

Then a black gelding to his right snorted from the shadows and startled the deputy. Baker looked at the horse and stared at it. The animal was tethered to a tree. He wondered why the horse had been seemingly abandoned just outside the livery stable.

It made no sense to the young lawman.

Baker rested a hand on the weathered wood of the side of the wagon and returned his attention to the frosty ground. As he did so, his eyes noticed something a few feet from his crushed cigarette stub.

The deputy stepped backward and then knelt.

The light from the livery stable glinted off the frost-covered sand. His eyes tightened as they observed what looked like crimson rubies. His fingers automatically touched them, but they were not precious jewels at all, but something far more disturbing. He stared at his fingertips and brought them close to his face. As his fingers and thumb rubbed together, he realized his digits were smeared in blood.

'Blood,' he muttered drily.

Baker glanced up at the wide open stable doors as his mind raced. Everything Dobie had taught his less experienced deputy simply vanished from his thoughts. The sheriff had always told him never to head into potential danger alone, but Baker could not recall a solitary word his mentor had said.

'What the hell is going on around here?' he asked himself curiously. 'Men don't just spill blood and then vanish into thin air.'

The deputy could see the blacksmith working hard on the tall grey stallion in the centre of the livery. He slowly rose to his full height and rubbed his fingers down his top coat.

Something just did not add up in the young lawman's mind.

He gritted his teeth and then lifted his heavy coat and pushed it behind his holstered gun. He checked the weapon and then slid it back into its leather pouch.

'Something's damn fishy around here and I intend finding out what it is,' Baker took a deep breath and then advanced toward the large open barn doors. The stories Dobie had told him about the notorious Fire Wolf filled his young mind but they did not slow his determined pace. He had mustered every scrap of his courage and would not allow fear to stop him.

Baker entered the brightly illuminated livery stable and paused about six feet behind the broad back of the muscular blacksmith.

The deputy knew that he was no gunslinger and might never be able to draw his holstered gun as swiftly as any of the men who earned their dubious livelihoods with their weaponry, so he rested his hand on the gun grip.

'What you want, Slim?' Tor asked the deputy without even turning to see the terrified lawman. 'If you're looking for Fire Wolf he left about twenty minutes back.'

Baker was startled.

'How'd you know it was me, Tor?' he nervously asked the sweat-covered man. 'You ain't got eyes where a man ain't meant to have eyes, have you?'

Tor turned away from the injured horse he had just stitched up with catgut and stared at the confused deputy who still held on to his holstered gun.

'Hell, I spotted you when you got to the wagon, son,' the blacksmith replied before inspecting his handiwork and patting the tall grey. 'I thought it was Fire Wolf returning for something.'

121

Baker's eyes darted around the huge stable in a vain search for the notorious hired gun.

'Where is he, Tor?' he asked as he slowly advanced across the straw-covered floor toward the burly man. 'Where's Fire Wolf?'

Tor Olsen placed a hand on the shoulder of the deputy and gave the younger man a fatherly look.

'Believe me, Slim,' he said. 'You don't wanna go up against the likes of Fire Wolf.'

Baker looked offended.

'Why not?'

Tor sighed heavily and shook his head. Droplets of sweat flew in all directions from bald head. He smiled.

'Why not?' He repeated the deputy's question and led the stallion toward an empty stall.

'Yeah, why not, Tor?' Baker asked.

The blacksmith backed the tall grey into the stall and hung a feed bag over the stallion's nose so it could eat. He then walked toward the deputy and picked up the metal bucket of bloody water. He looked at Baker.

'Coz he'll surely kill you, Slim,' the blacksmith informed the novice lawman. 'That's why not. Stay clear of that varmint if you wanna stay healthy.'

FIFTEEN

After making their way through the labyrinth of dark alleys that encroached the ramshackle buildings surrounding the high-sided livery stable, the wounded Joel Majors led his silent companion in through the back of one of abandoned structures nearby. He closed and bolted the door behind them and then pulled a box of matches from his pants pocket. Fire Wolf said nothing as he stood beside the door as the younger man struck a match and touched the wick of a lamp set in the middle of a wooden table. He replaced its glass funnel and blew the match out.

The light in the room grew as Majors turned its brass wheel and allowed the notorious Fire Wolf to observe the derelict interior. The deadly man in black rested his hands on his gun grips and watched as the younger man sat down on one of the four chairs dotted around the table.

Fire Wolf studied the small room. There was another door behind the table but nothing else.

'Where the hell am I, Majors?' Fire Wolf asked as

he removed the cigar from his lips and handed it to his seated companion. 'You can finish this. The smoke will take your mind off the pain that graze is giving you.'

Joel Majors took the cigar and drew in smoke. He then looked carefully at the tall figure before him and slowly exhaled. He had heard of Fire Wolf but had never truly believed any of the stories linked to him.

Until now.

'This is just one of the abandoned houses Jeb James owns, Fire Wolf,' he said as he painfully sucked in more smoke from the cigar. 'This part of town is full of them. Mostly abandoned like this 'un.'

Fire Wolf nodded and then looked down on Majors. Whatever he was feeling, he was keeping to himself. There was not one hint of emotion in his hardened features as his wrists rested upon his guns.

'That's mighty interesting, but why d'you bring me here, Majors?' he snarled through gritted teeth as he paced around the table like a caged cougar seeking a route to escape by. 'And who the hell do you want me to kill?'

Major gripped the cigar with his teeth. 'I wouldn't be so eager to earn the money in that envelope, Fire Wolf. This ain't no ordinary killing you've bin hired for.'

'Is that so?' Fire Wolf drawled in a low ominous tone.

'I got me a feeling that you'll be handing that envelope back when you find out the details of the job,' Majors said and inhaled more of the soothing smoke. 'I reckon that even someone as good at killing as you are will shy away from this job.'

Fire Wolf raised an eyebrow. 'I've never chickened out of a killing job in my entire life, sonny. They ain't invented the job that's too big for me yet.'

Majors held his tender side. The blacksmith had stitched him up before finishing working on the grey stallion, but the wound was still raw and painful. He turned and looked at the man in black as the tall figure moved around the table.

'I'm not sure anyone can fulfil this job, Fire Wolf,' he stated from behind a cloud of cigar smoke. 'Not even you.'

Fire Wolf frowned.

'If anyone requires killing,' he snorted. 'I can kill them, boy. Now why don't you spill the beans and tell me who you want killing? The sooner I know the sooner I can do it.'

The youngster looked up through the smoke that filtered through his teeth. Beads of sweat trailed down his face from his mane of damp hair.

'I ain't the one who hired you, Fire Wolf,' he explained. 'I just got the job to deliver the money and bring you here. If I'd known that you were gonna shoot me, I'd have turned the job down.'

Fire Wolf stopped abruptly behind Majors.

'You ain't the varmint that hired me?' he asked with a tone of disbelief in his voice.

'Nope,' Majors replied. 'I ain't got that kinda money, Fire Wolf.'

'Then who is the cowardly varmint that gets young-
sters to do his dirty work for him, boy?' Fire Wolf
growled angrily from behind the seated man. 'Why
didn't he have the guts to show up himself?'

Before Majors could reply, the door behind the
infamous hired killer creaked as its door knob was
turned. Fire Wolf swung around on his heels and
drew both his .45s and cocked their hammers.

'I'm the coward that hired you, Fire Wolf,' a shaky
voice uttered from the blackness beyond the door as
it gradually opened.

Instinctively Fire Wolf aimed both his six-shooters
at the feeble voice. His fingers itched as they curled
around the triggers. Every sinew in his tall lean frame
wanted to fire his weapons, but somehow he resisted
the overwhelming temptation. He stepped to the
side of the seated Majors and watched the shadowy
figure inch his way into the lamp light. The strange
sound of tapping on the flagstones intrigued the last
of the Mandan. Fire Wolf was unsure what the noise
actually was, but was still ready to blast his weapons if
he did not like what he was about to see.

'Stay calm, Fire Wolf,' the brittle voice said.

Fire Wolf inhaled deeply, 'I'm always calm. Just
keep walking toward me. I wanna see what a coward
looks like up close.'

The man who entered the small room looked
about seventy years of age, but in truth he was far
younger. He required two walking sticks just to
remain upright. Their metal tips tapped on the
ground as though signalling his every step. He slowly

126

made his way into the lamp light and tentatively walked to a vacant chair.

'I'm sorry you got hurt, Joel,' he said to Majors.

'That's OK,' the youngster nodded.

Fire Wolf narrowed his eyes. He had not expected to see anyone, let alone such a broken shell of a man as this. He watched as the wreckage of a man eased himself down next to Majors and sighed heavily.

The man finally looked up at Fire Wolf and nodded.

'There was a time when I was able to do anything I needed done by myself,' the fragile man muttered. 'Nowadays I need other folks' help. That ain't easy for someone like me, Fire Wolf.'

Fire Wolf returned his six-guns to their holsters and rubbed his smooth jawline thoughtfully. He pulled out a chair and sat down as his eyes burned across the distance between himself and the old man. The lamplight flickered across their very different features.

The last of the Mandan stared at the older man.

'You hired me?' he asked as he plucked the cigar from Majors' lips and took a long drag on it before ramming it back into the stunned youngster's mouth. He allowed the strong smoke to fester for a while before exhaling. 'You sure don't look like the type of galoot who hires folks like me.'

The elderly man gave a slight smile.

'My name is Quincy LaRue,' he sighed and looked at Fire Wolf with watery eyes. 'I have never done any wrong to anyone in my entire life. This is not what I would normally even consider, but something that has been forced upon me.'

'I don't understand, LaRue,' Fire Wolf muttered.

LaRue rested his elbows on the surface of the table and stared at the hired killer. His expression was one that Fire Wolf had never seen in the face of any of those who had hired his lethal skills before.

It was guilt.

'Jeb James hides many secrets behind the walls of his fortress home, Fire Wolf,' LaRue explained sadly. 'He might have built this town and grown rich over the years, but he is no saintly benefactor.'

Fire Wolf's face showed no emotion.

'What has he done that has riled you up to want him dead, LaRue?' he asked. 'I don't normally ask any questions, but for some reason this don't seem exactly normal to me.'

LaRue stared at the hardened features of the man he had just had Majors hire on his behalf. Unlike Fire Wolf, his entire face was a cauldron of mixed emotions.

'Jeb James and his hired army of misfits have done anything they wanted here over the years, Fire Wolf,' he stated as he held both walking sticks with one hand between his legs. 'Most of the old timers in and around Jamesburg have tended to turn a blind eye to it. I'm ashamed to say that I was one of them. I always figured that if it didn't directly affect me, then I didn't give a damn. I was wrong.'

Fire Wolf leaned back on his chair and stared hard at the man who appeared more dead than alive. It was the first time he had taken any interest in the motives of those who hired him to do their killing for them.

'So Jeb James and his hired guns hurt you, LaRue?' he asked.

Quincy LaRue sighed heavily.

'In a way,' he explained. 'They never even tried to do anything to me and mine when I was whole. When I was fit and strong they stayed clear, but after my accident when I ended up like this, they got cocky.'

'What you mean?' Fire Wolf leaned forward and frowned.

'They started rustling my steers and running my cowhands off, but I could cope with that,' LaRue inhaled and steadied himself as he drew close to the climax of his torrid tale. 'Then they raided my ranch and kidnapped my daughter.'

Fire Wolf's expression changed.

'They took your daughter?' He looked surprised at the course the story was taking.

LaRue gave a nod of his head. The light of the lamp revealed the tears rolling down the broken man's face as he mustered up every ounce of his composure to finish his harrowing story.

'They blatantly came to my ranch in the middle of the night and kidnapped my lovely Jenny,' he sobbed. 'Jeb James laughed in my face as they dragged her screaming out of my ranch house and took her to the fortress. My dear wife was so upset she passed away shortly afterwards. If I'd still been a real man, they would never have dared, but as you can see, I ain't a real man any more.'

Fire Wolf stared hard at the man who was not just physically broken but also mentally close to the edge. He pushed his hand into his jacket pocket and extracted a long cigar and placed it between his teeth. He bit off its tip and spat the tiny tobacco remnant at the floor.

'When was this?' he asked as he pulled out a match and scratched it with his thumbnail.

'A month back,' LaRue answered.

Fire Wolf raised the match to the cigar and puffed. 'Why would James want your daughter, LaRue?'

Quincy LaRue looked at Fire Wolf and shrugged. He could not answer the simple question because it was too awful for him to admit possible. He pulled a handkerchief from his pocket and covered his pained expression.

Fire Wolf knew exactly why men of any colour or creed took female hostages as he had witnessed it many times during his youth. He had seen many of his tribe's young womenfolk snatched from his encampment. It was only much later that he discovered the many reasons for such actions.

None of them sat well with him.

'I guess you don't just want Jeb James killed, do you?' he asked. 'His hired help don't sound much better than him.'

'I can't afford for you to kill more than one man, Fire Wolf,' LaRue swallowed hard.

'Forget about the money,' Fire Wolf muttered

through his cigar smoke. 'Sometimes I've been known to kill just for the sheer fun of it.'

LaRue leaned over the expanse of table between them.

'I'm desperate to find out if my Jenny is still alive, Fire Wolf,' he said. 'I tried to get the sheriff to find out, but he's no better than the sentries that protect James. The sheriff just laughed at me and told me to forget about it. How can a father forget his only child?'

Fire Wolf stood to his full height. He paced around the table and chairs, silently leaving a shoulder-high cloud of smoke in his wake. He then paused and looked down at the crippled man who watched his every action.

'I don't normally do anything apart from killing folks, but I reckon this ain't exactly my normal kind of job,' he said through a cloud of cigar smoke. He patted the swollen envelope tucked inside his breast pocket. 'This money will cover the whole thing no matter how many varmints I have to kill. If your daughter is still alive, I'll find her. '

Majors looked up at the man in black. 'I'll tag along with you if you need my help, Fire Wolf,' he volunteered.

Fire Wolf showed no emotion as he nodded to his wounded companion. His volatile mind was already planning something that was far beyond his usual practices. He tilted his head and stared at the far younger man.

'I might just require your help, Majors,' he muttered as he considered the task he was contemplating. 'This could be the kinda job which needs a distraction or two. I reckon you might be able to distract a few of them hired guns just long enough for me to do what I gotta do.'

'Do you have a plan?' Majors gasped as he studied the lean figure. 'Already?'

Fire Wolf shrugged. Something was indeed fermenting inside his fertile mind but he was unsure of what exactly it was. That, he thought, would take a little longer to pin down.

'I'm working on it,' he eventually said.

For the first time since his daughter had been forcibly taken from his ranch by Jeb James and his men, LaRue felt optimistic that there was a chance his beloved Jenny might be rescued.

'You think that you could rescue my daughter, Fire Wolf?' LaRue asked the mysterious hired killer. 'Do you?'

Fire Wolf had never witnessed anything to match the glowing smile which suddenly beamed from the face of the crippled man before him. He moved to LaRue and silently patted his bony shoulder.

Quincy LaRue looked up at the deadly infamous gunman.

'You're a good man,' he said.

Fire Wolf gave a shake of his head. 'Nope I ain't. I'm a hired killer. I just don't cotton to folks doing as they damn well please simply because they've got money.'

'It'll be damn dangerous, son. Nobody has ever managed to breach those defences that Jeb James has surrounded himself with,' he warned the mysterious Mandan. 'For more than twenty years folks have failed to get inside that fortress unless they've been invited.'

The ruthless killer sighed heavily through a cloud of cigar smoke, leaned over and whispered into LaRue's ear.

'I will,' Fire Wolf vowed.

SIXTEEN

The final hours of darkness still reigned supreme over the now-quiet streets of Jamesburg as the pair of outlaws guided their lathered-up mounts on to the ridge and drew rein. Both Holden and Allen looked around the now quiet town and hovered above their horses. Holden rubbed his gloved knuckle across his teeth and began to doubt the wisdom of his notion of trying to bushwhack the man who had killed their fellow gang members hours earlier.

'You don't look so damn cocky now, Lane,' Allen noted as he rested his hands on his saddle horn. 'If you were right and it was the notorious Fire Wolf that killed our boys, I got me a feeling that he's got the edge on us.'

'What you mean?' Holden snapped as his nerves began to fray in doubt. 'I ain't scared of the critter who gunned down Bart and the boys. Like I told you earlier, all we gotta do is a bit of sniffing and find him.'

'And kill him,' Allen added.

134

'Yep, and then we kill the varmint,' Holden nodded firmly.

'How do we know when the critter has bin paid, Lane?' Allen posed as he leaned his aching back against his saddle cantle. 'I doubt if he'll make it public knowledge.'

Holden swung his horse around and stared hard into the moonlit face of his companion. He raised a finger and pointed it straight at the exhausted face of Allen.

'First we gotta locate the critter,' he snarled. 'Once we got his sorrowful hide in our gun sights, we'll figure out the rest.'

'I don't give a damn about this Fire Wolf *hombre*,' Ben Allen was dog-tired and not ashamed who knew it. He yawned and turned his horse. 'All I wanna do is find a bed and sleep for the next two weeks.'

Holden steered his horse next to his partner.

'I've heard that Fire Wolf gets maybe five or ten thousand bucks to do someone else's killing, Ben,' he said for the umpteenth time. 'Think about it. That's real money and if we crossed the border into Mexico, we could live like kings with that much money.'

'Maybe,' Allen sighed and indicated with a nod of his head for his partner to look through the blackness that had enveloped this part of the town. 'Look yonder, Lane.'

Holden momentarily stood in his stirrups and saw what Allen had spotted beyond the ramshackle buildings that dominated this section of the sleeping town. The sight of the tall livery stable stood out from the rest of the structures due to the lantern light which still flooded from its massive open doors.

'We'll take the nags over there and get them fed and watered, Ben,' he said as he tapped his spurs into the flanks of his flagging animal. 'Then we'll find a hotel and get some shuteye ourselves.'

Allen pointed at the canvas bags tied behind their cantles.

'What about these?' he said nervously. 'They got the name of the bank we robbed printed on them. We can't go flashing them around or we'll have the law hunting us before we got a chance to kill that hired gun.'

Holden shook his head as both horses made their way across the rough ground toward the inviting livery stable. As they neared the massive structure, he glanced at his partner.

'Pull on them leathers, Ben,' he said as he stopped his own horse and dismounted.

Allen watched as Holden stooped two handfuls of the damp sand off the ground and started to rub the canvas vigorously until the betraying words were obliterated from prying view. Holden then repeated the action and smothered more of the frosty sand over the canvas bank bag behind Allen's cantle.

'That should do it,' Holden said as he rubbed his hands together. Then as he was about to grab his long leathers again his keen eyes noticed the blood beside the upturned wagon. He stared at it as he pulled a cigar from his jacket pocket and pushed it into the corner of his mouth.

As Holden struck a match and lit his cigarette, Allen wondered what had caught his cohort's attention.

'What you seen, Lane?' he asked.

Holden tossed the match at the bloody droplets. Its flame was extinguished by the frost. A sliver of smoke trailed upward as both men watched.

With a point of his cigar, Holden indicated at the hardly noticeable blood on the frost-covered surface of the sandy ground.

'Somebody got themselves shot by here, Ben,' he muttered through the smoke which peppered his words as he spoke. The outlaw glanced around the dark area which surrounded them and the stable building.

Allen rubbed his neck.

'Looks like our old friend Fire Wolf has bin here, Lane,' he muttered anxiously as he too stared around them for any hint of the legendary gunman. 'Maybe we'd best get these horses bedded down and find that hotel.'

'Good idea, Ben.' Holden grabbed his reins and led his horse toward the tall barn doors and the bright light that emanated from the structure's interior. When they were less than a dozen feet from the massive livery stable, Allen threw his leg over the tail of his mount and lowered himself down.

'I'll untie these bags, Lane.'

'Good idea,' Holden sucked on smoke as his eyes darted around the shadowy ground outside the

livery. Just as he was about to draw more cigar smoke
into his lungs, Holden heard the hefty footsteps of
the blacksmith approaching from the heart of the
livery.

Tor Olsen stopped walking when he saw the two
trail-weary outlaws and studied them as he rested his
massive hands on his wide hips.

'Howdy, gents,' he greeted them. 'If them nags are
looking for some tender-hearted care, bring them
in.'

Allen hoisted both the canvas bags on to his shoulders as his partner led the horses toward the
muscular blacksmith. Tor took the long leathers
from Holden and led the animals toward some
vacant stalls.

Holden glanced around the interior of the livery
nervously and then looked at the blacksmith as he
expertly loosened the cinch straps and hauled the
saddles free of the weary animals' backs.

'Kinda late for you to be working, ain't it?' Holden
remarked as he withdrew his cigar and tapped its ash
on to the straw-covered ground.

Tor rested both saddles on the stall walls and then
peeled the horses' blankets off their back and placed
them close to his hot forge.

'Yep, it is kinda late for me to be working,' he
agreed as he filled two buckets from his water barrel
and placed them in front of the horses. 'I've bin real
busy. I had to tend that tall grey over in the end stall.
He needed sewing up.'

The outlaws glanced at the horse and then back at

the blacksmith as he filled two feed bags with oats and carried them toward their mounts.

'That stallion was knifed?' Holden queried.

Tor nodded as he waited for the horses to finish their long-awaited drink before he hung the feed bags on them. He stared at the two trail-weary outlaws and smiled.

'Do you know what happened to the cowpokes that knifed that handsome horse?' he asked as he strode back to his forge and sat on its brick rim.

Both outlaws shook their heads.

'They got shot and killed,' Tor informed them.

Holden tilted his head as he chewed on his cigar. 'Who'd shoot and kill men for just knifing a horse?'

The blacksmith rested his massive hands on his knees and leaned forward toward the two strangers. His eyes twinkled in the forge light.

'You ever heard of a varmint named Fire Wolf?' he asked.

Both Holden and Allen slowly nodded.

SEVENTEEN

Black ominous storm clouds spread across the vast heavens and masked the stars and new moon from sending their eerie illumination down upon the sprawling settlement. A veil of dark shadows smothered the activity which moved like a rattler toward Jeb James' fortress home. The man in black sucked the last of his cigar's smoke from the twisted tobacco remnant and then tossed it aside as a crude plan suddenly began to formulate inside his mind. Both he and his injured companion walked steadily down the boardwalks in unified determination. Fire Wolf said nothing as his narrowed eyes glanced upward at the gathering clouds. For the first time since Majors had encountered the deadly hired killer, he saw a wry smile etch the man in black's hardened features.

'Looks like the Devil is on our side, Majors,' he drawled as he stretched up to his full height. 'I figure there's a storm brewing. That's just what we need to make my plan work.'

Joel Majors moved next to the imposing figure as they both continued to move steadily along the main street of Jamesburg.

'How can a storm help us, Fire Wolf?' he asked naively.

Fire Wolf sniffed at the air like a hound dog and paused beside the now quiet Buckweed saloon. The last of the Mandan looked over its swing doors into its interior. Only the bartenders remained clearing up the debris left by the night's customers. Fire Wolf inhaled deeply and then glanced at his companion before continuing along the main street.

'I smell thunder, Majors,' he said simply. 'Where there's thunder, there's usually lightning. The more lightning, the better the odds of our managing to rescue that young gal.'

'I don't understand,' Majors admitted.

Fire Wolf raised an arm. His left hand pointed across the wide street to the stage depot office. It was situated fifty feet from a stable where the Overland Stagecoach company kept their dozens of horses.

'How come they're burning the midnight oil?' he asked as his quicksilver mind began to consider a new plan. 'Both the depot and the stables are lit up like the fourth of July.'

'The stagecoach company runs twenty-four hours a day. There's always someone there,' Majors explained.

The man in black stepped off the boardwalk and crossed the street with the younger man on his heels. When Fire Wolf reached the office, he stared in through the window and then continued on to the stables.

Majors almost had to run in order to keep pace with the tall, silent hired gunman. Fire Wolf rounded the corner and marched through its open double doors. He did not stop until he reached one of the workers who was carefully buckling up a team of horses.

'Is there a stagecoach due?' Fire Wolf asked the sweat-soaked man stood between two fresh horses.

The man glanced up at the elegant figure before him and then spat at the ground. He flexed his muscular arms and looked Fire Wolf up and down.

'Why d'you wanna know?' he asked as a couple of his workmates joined him.

Fire Wolf pushed the tails of his black top coat over the ivory grips of his holstered weapons. His icy glare was threatening enough to loosen the tongue of the man.

'It ain't none of your business why I wanna know,' Fire Wolf drawled in a low growl. 'Just answer the question and you might live a tad longer. Is there a stagecoach due?'

The face of the burly man twitched.

'There's one due in about thirty minutes,' he reluctantly said. 'We're getting a team of fresh nags ready for it to continue on to Carson City.'

Fire Wolf nodded.

'There ain't no need for you to bust a gut working,' the man in black stated coldly. 'It won't need a fresh team.'

142

'How come?' the confused man asked.

Fire Wolf did not reply. He turned and walked to where the equally bewildered Majors was standing and led him back to the office. The deadly killer sat down on a bench outside the office and pulled out a cigar from his inside pocket.

'What was that about, Fire Wolf?' Majors asked as he sat down next to the man who had placed the cigar between his lips and produced a match from his vest pocket. 'What the hell is going on in that mind of yours?'

The match erupted into flame as Fire Wolf ran a thumbnail across it. He allowed the flame to settle and then brought it up to his cigar and puffed thoughtfully. He then tossed the blackened ember at the sand.

'It would be a crying shame to kill a fresh team of horses when the stagecoach already has a tuckered-out bunch dragging it here, boy,' Fire Wolf said calmly.

Majors was even more confused. 'What?'

Suddenly Fire Wolf leapt back to his feet and gripped the long tobacco stick between his teeth. He glanced at his young companion and dragged him upright.

'Where's the hardware store?' Fire Wolf asked.

Joel Majors blinked hard as a distant thunderclap rocked the sprawling settlement. He looked up at the blackening sky and then at Fire Wolf.

'There's a hardware store about a hundred yards away in a side street,' he revealed. 'Why?'

143

'Take me there,' Fire Wolf demanded. 'We've only got about thirty minutes to get this done.'

'But it'll be shuttered this time of the night,' Majors blurted at the gunman. 'There ain't nobody there.'

'Frankly, I don't give a damn,' Fire Wolf said. 'Open or closed, I'm getting what we need.'

'Exactly what do we need?' the younger man asked.

'Dynamite, Majors,' Fire Wolf replied drily. 'A whole mess of dynamite.'

EIGHTEEN

The heavily laden stagecoach moved through the worsening storm along the trail road out of Jamesburg. The mysterious Fire Wolf sat on the driver's board while his temporary cohort sat next to him and portrayed a shotgun guard. Rain lashed the high-sided vehicle as flashes of lightning peppered the black sky, yet the man in black seemed oblivious to anything apart from the fortress sat on the highest point of the long ridge.

Mercilessly, Fire Wolf cracked the long leathers across the backs of the exhausted team. After reaching the fork in the road, the deadly killer pulled the hefty reins to his chest as his right boot pressed hard on the stagecoach's brake-pole. Fire Wolf stared through the incessant downpour at the equally bedraggled Majors. To their right the trail continued on to the next town on the vehicle's itinerary while the trail to their left led up to the daunting home of Jeb James.

The normally arid terrain was swiftly reverting to a

mud bath, but that seemed to suit the expressionless Fire Wolf as he stared through the driving rain.

It had not taken much to persuade the stagecoach driver to hand over the reins of his vehicle. The sight of Fire Wolf holding his pair of matched .45s and a few golden eagles bribe had been enough to swing the transaction.

Had any of the stage depot workers realized exactly what the notorious man in black actually intended though, it might have been a different matter.

The hardware store had been a lot easier to do business with. Fire Wolf had simply kicked down its double doors and taken everything he wanted. After loading the interior of the stagecoach with box after box of dynamite sticks and fuse wire, the pair ascended the high platform and started their dangerous journey.

'The trail up the James ranch house is turning into a damn river, Fire Wolf,' Majors noted as he clung to the shotgun he had discovered in the driver's box before they had left the settlement. 'If we don't start up there pretty soon, we ain't gonna be able to.'

Fire Wolf looked down on the six-horse team and nodded.

'Get down and light them fuses I rigged, boy,' he commanded his younger companion as he gripped the heavy long leathers in readiness.

Joel Majors looked troubled by the thought of putting a match to the fuse wire. He knew that if Fire Wolf had miscalculated the length of the individual fuses, they would get themselves blown into tiny fragments that nobody would ever find.

'How long will them fuses take to burn down to the dynamite, Fire Wolf?' he asked as he prepared to descend from their high perch.

Fire Wolf looked through the rain at the younger man.

'Damned if I know,' he freely admitted. 'I'd wait until I get halfway up the slope before lighting them though. Just in case I figured it wrong. I'll signal you when to light them fuses. Don't forget to jump clear when you've lit them.'

'I ain't gonna forget that,' Majors grimaced and clambered down to the ground and then opened the carriage door and sat among the opened boxes. As he pulled the various lengths of fuse wire toward him, the stagecoach abruptly jerked back into action.

Majors located his box of dry matches from deep inside his jacket and exhaled as the long vehicle rocked back and forth and began the long climb toward the massive gates.

The stagecoach might have gotten bogged down or sunk in the muddy ground had Fire Wolf not steered the team of doomed horses off the slippery trail and on to the rougher terrain. The desert vegetation allowed both the horses' hoofs and the coach's wheels to find something to grip.

Deafening thunderclaps rocked everything beneath the black, angry clouds as lightning flashed across the devilish sky. Fire Wolf stared at the towers to either side of the massive and seemingly impenetrable gates. The man in black lashed the long leathers down on to the backs of the six horses and urged them ever onward.

As Fire Wolf continued on toward the high walled edifice, he noticed that there were no sentries to be seen. The mixture of relentless rain and nerve-shattering bolts of deadly lightning had frightened Jeb James' hired protectors and forced them to take cover.

That was exactly what he wanted.

When the stagecoach was within two hundred feet of the imposing wall, Fire Wolf grabbed the luggage rail and hung precariously over the side of the mud-splattered vehicle. He caught Majors' eye and signalled the youngster.

'Now,' he called out to his cohort.

Majors nodded and carefully struck a match and began lighting the many fuse wires. The wires immediately began to spit sparks in every direction as they quickly burned steadily down.

Fire Wolf drove the six-horse team up on to the ridge and positioned the massive stagecoach alongside the huge gates before wrapping his long reins around the brake pole. No sooner had the vehicle halted when Majors jumped out of the carriage and darted for the sparse undergrowth in search of cover.

The terrified younger man did not stop running until he found a ditch and then dropped into it. Majors' heart was pounding like a war drum inside his chest as he steadied himself and turned to look over the muddy rim of the ditch. To his horror, he saw something which he had not expected.

With the sparks of the fuse wires erupting from within the interior of the coach, Fire Wolf remained standing on the stagecoach roof.

Majors wanted to scream out at the man in black, but knew that if he did it might alert the sheltering sentries. He gripped the twin-barrelled shotgun in his hands and closed his eyes tightly. Majors wondered what the lethal hired killer was doing by remaining on top of a bomb.

What was Fire Wolf doing? The question repeatedly screamed inside Majors' head. Jump and run, his mind implored. Jump and run before it was too late. Then, after what seemed like an eternity of waiting for the explosion, Majors could not contain himself any longer. He got back to his feet just in time to see Fire Wolf jump from the roof of the stagecoach, grab at the wall and disappear over it.

Then a mere heartbeat later the stagecoach exploded like an erupting volcano. Majors was knocked off his feet and thrown backwards by the sheer force of the blast. As he lay on his back, the youngster stared in horror at the fiery plumes of crimson flames flying up into the black sky. It was like staring into the very bowels of Satan's lair. The boxes of dynamite sticks exploded in quick succession, shaking the ground he lay upon. Suddenly Majors noticed that it was not just raining water but debris of every shape, size and weight.

Large stones from the wall fell and bounced all around the startled onlooker. Then gigantic lumps of wood crashed into the muddy terrain. Majors scrambled to his feet and ran as fast as his legs could carry him through the slippery desert as the deafening crescendo continued.

After fleeing more than fifty feet away from the terrifying explosion, Majors slid to a halt and swung over on to his chest and cocked the shotgun hammers. He stared in disbelief to where only moments before he had seen the stagecoach beside the gates of the fortress.

As clouds of choking smoke swirled between himself and the brutalized wall, Majors gasped in awe at what he and Fire Wolf had achieved. Vicious flames rose from a deep pit which was still exploding as one by one the dynamite boxes exploded. Majors clutched the shotgun as his eyes vainly searched for any sign of Fire Wolf himself.

Yet all his red raw eyes could see were the mutilated bodies of the six horses that had taken the full force of the explosives they were carrying. Majors tried to swallow, but there was no spittle. He wanted to advance and follow Fire Wolf into the compound through the massive crater the hired killer had just created, but the continual blasts forced him to remain where he was.

Then, as his eyes darted along what remained of the walls and towers, he saw a couple of the stunned sentries staggering along the wall's parapet. Majors raised the shotgun and aimed at the heavily-armed guards.

He pulled on both triggers and watched as they took the full impact of his buckshot. As he pulled fresh shells from his pockets to reload his shotgun, his mind raced to thoughts of his mentor.

Where was Fire Wolf?

Was he still alive?

So many questions and not one positive answer.

NINETEEN

Fire Wolf had only just cleared the wall and dropped into the courtyard when the stagecoach exploded. The man in black had been lifted off his feet and thrown like a ragdoll toward the large house. One of the Gatling guns had been torn from its placement on top of the gate tower and landed less than six feet from him. Its sturdy brass construction had somehow survived the devilish flight. Fire Wolf clambered back to his feet and dragged the lethal repeating gun upright as three of James' guards came running from their bunkhouse with their Winchesters in their hands. They raced toward the destroyed gates and wall.

The sentries had only been twenty feet away from where he stood when they realized that the figure in the long black trail coat was not one of their number. The men turned their rifles on Fire Wolf and started firing.

The sound of the Gatling gun spraying its deadly bullets as Fire Wolf turned its handle echoed around the compound. Bullets spewed from its barrel in rapid succession as the last of the Mandan unleashed the weapon's fury.

The sentries were ripped to shreds. Blood and lumps of flesh flew in all directions as Fire Wolf turned the barrel from side to side and cranked its handle.

As the lifeless bodies hit the sand, the expressionless man in black walked away from the smoking brass weapon, pushed his coat tails over his holsters and continued on toward the house. As Fire Wolf reached the front of the once-imposing structure, he noticed that the initial dynamite blast had shattered every one of its windows.

Fire Wolf drew his guns and fired at the door. His perfect aim hit the lock and shattered it. He followed his bullets and kicked the door off its hinges. His unblinking eyes stared into the cavernous interior as he cocked his hammers again.

'Where are you, James?' Fire Wolf yelled out as he stood in the hall. He was about to advance when he heard running behind his wide shoulders. He spun on his heels just as another of Jeb James' henchmen came racing out of the large courtyard and into the hall behind him.

Without a moment's hesitation, Fire Wolf squeezed on his triggers. Two plumes of blinding venom spewed from his gun barrels and hit the sentry in his guts. The man crumpled lifelessly on to the floor.

Fire Wolf swiftly returned his attention to the interior of the house and moved silently down the hall with his smoking guns jutting out at hip level. His thumbs hauled back on his gun hammers again as he neared the large library to his left.

The brightly illuminated interior of the building shook with each successive explosion that erupted from what was left of the stagecoach. Fire Wolf paused and glared into the room.

'Are you in here, James?' he taunted as he slowly stepped into the book-filled room. His eyes searched every corner of the large room as he slowly advanced deeper into the library. The only sound was from window glass as it crushed under his boots. 'Show yourself.'

The tall Mandan lowered his head and listened intently.

He could hear and see more than most men ever thought possible. His every honed instinct drew his full attention to a corner where a well-padded leather chair stood.

Fire Wolf slowly raised his guns and levelled them at the chair. Without a moment's hesitation, he fired. The bullets carved through the backrest of the chair and found their hidden target. The scent of burning padding filled the room as wisps of smoke trailed out of the blackened bullet holes in the chair.

The lethal killer cocked his hammers again and started to approach the chair as Jeb James suddenly stood up from behind it. Fire Wolf halted and watched as the wealthy rancher moved slowly out from his hiding place.

Blood covered James's shirt front.

154

'You done killed me,' he exclaimed. 'Why?'

'I was hired to kill you,' Fire Wolf smirked and then squeezed his triggers again. The shots hit the bewildered rancher in the throat and sent him crashing into a bookcase. As he fell to the ground, scores of tomes tumbled off its shelves and covered the body.

The hired killer had completed half of what he had told the elderly LaRue he would do. Now he had to try and discover whether the man's daughter was still alive.

Fire Wolf holstered his smoking .45s and marched back into the hall. His keen hearing detected the pathetic sobbing of a female coming from somewhere at the top of the staircase. His long legs raced up the carpeted steps until he located where the sound was coming from.

He unlocked the door and pushed it inward.

The sight which met his ice cold eyes caused Fire Wolf to hesitate. He suddenly began to wonder what other devilish outrages Jeb James had hidden within the walls of his grand home. The virtually naked female was spread-eagled on a bed. Her wrists and ankles were tied with leather laces to the ornate brass bedposts. He rushed to her and then pulled a bed sheet to cover her modesty.

'Are you Jenny LaRue?' he asked.

She nodded as if terrified of speaking.

'Ain't no call you being scared any longer,' Fire Wolf said. 'Jeb James ain't gonna hurt you or anyone else.'

Suddenly her fears vanished. 'How can you be sure?'

'I just killed the evil *hombre*, ma'am.' Fire Wolf pulled a knife from his belt and cut through the leather straps which bound her. He then wrapped her in the bedsheet and scooped her up in his arms. He then exited the room and carried her down the stairs.

'Where are you taking me?' Jenny LaRue asked her expressionless saviour as Fire Wolf ran out into the courtyard with her nestling into his shoulder.

'I'm taking you home, gal,' Fire Wolf said as his narrowed eyes watched Joel Majors clamber through the rubble and head toward them.

As she clung tightly to Fire Wolf, she whispered. 'There are lots of guards around here. Be careful.'

He looked into her tear-stained eyes.

'I already killed all of them too, ma'am,' he announced.

Fire Wolf looked at the breathless Majors.

'I can hear horses out behind the house, boy,' he drawled at the younger man. 'Saddle a couple of them so we can take this little gal home to see her pa.'

FINALE

Fire Wolf was alone as he steered his newly acquired mount through the streets of Jamesburg as the sun slowly rose and bathed everything in its light. He had delivered Jenny LaRue back to her father and was returning to check on his grey stallion before renting a hotel room for the night. As the man in black turned into the main street on his way to the livery stable, something caught his eye.

He noticed the two lawmen standing shoulder to shoulder beneath the porch overhang of their office. As both Dobie and his deputy spotted the unmistakable hired killer riding toward them, the older man drew his six-gun and aimed it at Fire Wolf.

'Hold it right there, sonny,' Dobie said firmly.

Fire Wolf allowed the horse to stop beside the hitching pole outside the office and then raised his arms. He was neither scared or surprised by the actions of anyone who wore a tin star.

'What you want, Sheriff?' he asked drily.

'Throw them guns down or I'll shoot,' Dobie said

nervously as he ventured to the edge of the board-walk and stared at the expressionless face of the last of the Mandan.

'I can't do that, Sheriff.' Fire Wolf tilted his head and looked beyond the shaking lawman. Baker wondered what Fire Wolf was taking such an interest in.

'What you looking at, Fire Wolf?' the deputy asked.

Without answering, Fire Wolf swung on his saddle and drew both his guns. He blasted up at an open hotel window on the opposite side of the street.

Sheriff Dobie watched in surprised horror as both Lane Holden and Ben Allen came falling out of the hotel room. Their blood-stained bodies rolled across the wooden shingled porch roof and then crashed into the sand. Their guns slowly followed and landed behind the lifeless outlaws.

'I'd holster that gun, Sheriff,' Baker suggested as Fire Wolf turned back around to face the lawmen.

'I'd listen to that young deputy. It sure sounds like a damn good idea to me, Sheriff,' the man in black said.

'Put the coffee on, Slim,' The seasoned lawman slid his six-shooter back into its holster and wiped the sweat off his rugged features. He swallowed and then raised a shaking finger to the mounted man in black. 'How'd you know them two was aiming to kill you, boy. You had your damn back to them.'

Fire Wolf gathered up his reins and pointed at the office window behind Dobie.

'I seen their reflections, Sheriff,' he drily said. 'I

figured they were either trying to kill me or you.'

Dobie went ashen. 'I could have shot you when you swung around, Fire Wolf. That was a mighty big risk to take.'

Fire Wolf tugged his reins and pulled his mount away from the hitching pole. He shook his head and pulled the brim of his Stetson down to shield his eyes from the rising sun.

'Not with that gun,' he stated. 'You could have squeezed on that trigger until I was as old as you are and the damn thing wouldn't fire. You hadn't cocked its hammer. '

Dobie blinked hard. 'I knew that, you cocky young buzzard.'

'I'm sure you did, Sheriff,' Fire Wolf tapped his spurs and started the horse trotting. 'If anyone wants me I'll be in the livery checking my horse. Later on I'll be in the hotel. I understand they've just got a vacancy.'

'You can't just gun down folks and ride away, boy,' Dobie shouted as the horse continued down the road in the direction of the livery stable. 'That ain't the way things is done in these parts.'

Fire Wolf looked over his shoulder at the irate sheriff.

'I'd check your Wanted posters, if I was you,' he called out. 'You and that deputy must have a few dollars coming your way for killing those two *hombres*.'

Sheriff Dobie raised his eyebrows. 'Reward money? Don't you wanna claim it, Fire Wolf?'

Fire Wolf shook his head.

'I ain't no stinking bounty hunter, Sheriff,' he said as he turned the corner and disappeared from sight.

Dobie was just about to head into his office to check his Wanted posters when a cowboy came galloping into town astride a lathered-up sorrel. He hastily dismounted and rushed to the lawman's side and whispered in the sheriff's ear. The sheriff looked at the cowboy as he threw his slender frame back on to his horse and continued on down the street.

Baker stepped out into the morning sun and looked at the face of the troubled lawman. 'What's wrong, Sheriff?'

Dobie looked at his deputy.

'Jeb James and every one of his hired guns are dead, Slim,' he stammered. 'That big wall surrounding his ranch house has been destroyed as well. '

Without uttering a word, both Dobie and Baker glanced to where they had last seen Fire Wolf riding down the street. They then looked at each other and then shrugged their shoulders.

'Do you reckon Fire Wolf had something to do with any of that, Sheriff?' Baker finally managed to ask his superior.

Dobie pressed his hand into the small of his deputy's back and pushed him into the office.

'Make that coffee, Slim,' the lawman stuttered. 'Make that coffee.'